shambles

D.M. O'NEAL

Cover design by Michelle Fairbanks / Fresh Design

Edited by Twyla Beth Lambert

Print ISBN 978-1-945419-28-7

ePub ISBN 978-1-945419-29-4

Library of Congress Control Number 2018941782

To my Hap… Steve Noonkester: A big man with a bigger heart. I learned of your death today. Your deep hearty laugh will be forever missed. May the demons of your past lay forever concealed, and your angels fly for all to see. Thank you for awakening me during a difficult time.

—November 28, 2007

sham•bles (shăm'bəlz) plural noun (used with a sing. verb)

A scene or condition of complete disorder or ruin. Great clutter or jumble; a total mess. A place or scene of bloodshed or carnage. A scene or condition of great devastation. A slaughterhouse: *Archaic* A meat market or butcher shop.

"*P*adre, I am an old woman, no?" The subject of my age usually elicits disbelief. I've always looked younger than my years, although of late, not so much. The constant worry and diminishing time age me.

Father Galindo replies as I expect. "No Señora, you are a *mature*, beautiful woman. I would not say old." Taking a handkerchief from his pocket, he wipes the sweat under his stiff collar and then his brow. We stroll along the gravel walkway from his dusty sedan to the house.

"I'll be seventy years old tomorrow," I state with elegance.

Aqua paint chips float on a warm breeze as the screen door slams shut behind us. The porch's ceiling fan wobbles a clattering tune, doing little to dissipate the humidity. I've grown accustomed to the heat in my self-imposed prison.

A spindly wooden chair creaks with the Padre's weight. "I know...." Taking the sweaty glass I offer, he sips with a bright smile and continues. "And your *nietos* will soon arrive for the Fiesta Grande." He motions toward the men stringing lights in trees bordering an immaculately manicured lawn. The postcard-perfect emerald vision spills out to the radiant sea.

"How long have we known each other?" My jaws tingle as

tart lemonade tempers the sweetness of the cookie dissolving on my tongue.

"Oh, *déjeme pensar*, since I returned to the island eight years ago." He dabs the cloth to his forehead again.

A large green beetle catches the Padre's attention as it creeps across the screen between us and the workers. The young man's black eyes focus on the bug while he calculates the length of our association.

He doesn't remember. We actually met when I arrived on the island twenty-eight years ago. He was just a boy. Father José Canales Galindo requested to serve the church on the island of his birth soon after completing seminary. I've known three priests since I began attending the Iglesias de San Miguel, and there's a good chance José will be the last.

I'm not Catholic, but none of the priests or neighbors ever questioned me about religion or more than polite generalities about my past. Taking a regular seat in Saint Michael's has prepared me for the inevitable day I will confess my sins, as I promised a dying man I would.

"Have you ever known me to be unkind or ruthless?" Although my question begs reassurance, his saintly resemblance to Jesus in chinos provokes doubt. Can I trust him?

"Ruthless? I do not know the meaning of this word, ruthless."

"It means evil, Father, bad... *muy mal*." I lay a hand on his forearm, my pale skin in stark contrast to his, smooth and auburn.

He looks intently at my frail hand and places his on top. "No, no Señora Brooks—you have always been good and generous to the Iglesias and the people of San Miguel. Why do you ask me these things?"

"I need to know that I can trust you. Trust you with something... something very personal." I sit tall and twist loose tendrils of gray hair into an untidy knot, waiting for his reaction.

"Of course, Señora. I am your priest. You can trust me with

anything." A deep wrinkle forms between his eyebrows. "What is it? A possession, or perhaps a secret?" A sly smile erupts. I wish the gift of a simple possession could bring peace. If only a precious jewel or cursed talisman dropped in his lap could free my conscience. Perhaps he thinks I am seeking atonement for infidelity or coming clean on a past thievery. I wish it were that uncomplicated. His naïve benevolence seems worthy of my trust.

"Only a possession of the heart, Father. I made a promise long ago, a promise I must keep before I die." I pause at his visible concern, pulling at the hem of my blouse.

"Are you ill? Do you want me to hear a final confession?"

"No, I'm not ill, but the time has come for me to return to the States. I want to be with my family in my final days. I've missed so much of their lives." Buried fear raises my tone. I turn away and stand to hide flushed cheeks.

"I will certainly miss… my life here." Clearing my throat, I continue. "This beautiful place, with its beautiful people…." I've postponed a confession long enough. I've made a prison of this paradise—and it's time I grant myself parole.

Rising, he consoles me with a gentle pat between my shoulders.

"I have a gift for the church, a large amount of money." I face him.

"Señora, you have already given the church so much." He hands me a paper napkin.

"Accepting the money is not conditional. I want you to understand that. Okay? Once I tell you what I have to tell you. You do what you feel you must. Okay?"

"Conditional?"

Unsure whether he's asking for a definition or an explanation, I push forward. "I have a story to tell. A story of long ago when I was a *young*, beautiful woman." I smile and brush a dark lock of hair from his forehead. A more familial gesture than our relationship warrants. "I need to tell someone what happened. Will you hear it?"

"*Si... por supuesto*. Of course I will, Señora Brooks."

With a deep sigh of relief, my shoulders relax and I stare through the screen door, beyond the iridescent bug and the dark-haired men to the ocean. To the north—to the life I left behind long ago.

FRIDAY, AUGUST 12, 1994, 2:30 A.M.

"We've got one, may be a suicide. Megan? You awake? Hello?" The gruff voice on the end of the line is a familiar one, my boss Sam.

"Yeah, yeah... sure." I reach for the lamp, click it on, sear my eyeballs with a forty-watt bulb. "Okay, on my way."

Adrenaline pumps as my feet hit the floor. I stumble over Alpha's outstretched furry carcass on my way to the bathroom. He raises his head and blinks at the sight of me sitting on the toilet. I rub my eyes and clear my head. There's no time for makeup or matching clothes. Do I wear shorts or pants? Is it indoors with air-conditioning or out in the smothering heat of another muggy Texas night? We never know this soon.

Honestly, it doesn't matter what I do at this point. Come daylight, I'll look like shit anyway. More than ready to stop drinking coffee and take the shower I'm not taking now. If it's a suicide, that's what I'll be doing; if not, I'll be there for God only knows how long, but I love it.

Punkin, Out again. Be back asap, Mom.

I tuck an edge of the note under the milk jug, the second place Connor will go when he wakes up. My old Accord bounces in reverse from the driveway and detours toward a stout cup of coffee at the Quik Sak.

I climb in the idling van waiting for me. "Male or female?"

"You know what I know." A harsh but familiar response from Sam and I don't take it personally. His fingers rake dirty hair from his forehead.

There's not much conversation between us en route. We live for each call out and make a good team, but at 3:00 a.m. we'd both rather be where we were at 2:00 a.m., asleep. Within an hour we'll be hard at work.

We turn the corner to see everyone waiting on us, the crime scene unit, to arrive. Blue and red lights whip the darkness. An officer lifts barrier tape stretched between mailboxes up over the van's windshield. With a silencing shush, it scrapes the roof. Sam weaves through police cars and pulls into the vacant spot reserved for us in front of the two-story brick house.

A crowd of men wait curbside beneath a cloud of smoke. A short, dark haired detective hollers. "Hey Sam, how ya been?" I know he doesn't expect an answer. Sam passes him with little more than a glance. He's not fond of the Napoleonic character. In Sam's opinion, Hernandez only made Detective due to the affirmative action policy within the Fort Worth Police Department. It certainly wasn't his performance.

"He's such a prick!" Sam says under his breath with a casual wave to the bothersome pest.

Conversation abruptly shifts to the oppressive heat wave, out of respect for me, the token female. Stopping a couple of paces behind Sam, like a faithful dog, I am disregarded in the obligatory chit-chat and handshakes. Unwilling to await my next command, I blurt out, "So what'd we have?" Anxious to get back to my bed, I refuse to be ignored.

"Well, darling!" A deep voice booms from above as a massive arm swings around me. The embrace cups my right shoulder in a sweaty underarm, then jerks the left in for a sideways hug. My shoulders feel the moist pressure. A mixture of smoke, body odor and day-old cologne fills my nostrils. I'm crazy about this man, Henry Able Parks. If I ever want a sugar daddy, he'll be my choice. I squeeze back, aware of the gun on his right hip.

Hap leans close, whispering in a slow drawl, "Ya better let go, Megan, before these yahoos get the wrong idea." We part. I suspect they've already got the wrong idea, and I don't care.

Hap became his initials after placing his mark on every item of evidence collected on crime scenes. It stuck even as he moved up the ranks in the department.

The three of us break from the pack to make our way up the pebbled walk. Hap briefs us with the details. "She's been here awhile... in full rigor. What would that be, five maybe eight hours in the air-conditioning? Husband says he found her just like this."

Sam pushes the door open as Hap points through the entryway to a woman's body suspended by a rope. The ligature is tied to a large, roughhewn cross timber above. The two men stop short of the threshold. Their abrupt halt leaves me to peer between masculine shoulders on tiptoe. The dangling corpse and an escaping cool draft from the house lends an impression of a well-decorated meat locker. The woman is clad in khaki shorts, a navy T-shirt and no shoes. Wispy strands of blonde hair cover her face. The two men step around the perimeter of the entryway, the porch light illuminating their way, to reach carpet. The slightest amount of dust could have left an identifiable footwear impression on the marble tile floor. They're mindful of every step, fearful of destroying evidence.

I follow behind them like an Indian tracker and notice the unnatural length of the woman's neck. Now I understand why it's called hangman's stretch. Her painted toenails rest a few inches from the newly upholstered dining chair from which she took her last step. I move toward the mantle to view pictures staggered one in front of the other. Young men in framed photographs, smiling happy faces, embrace in tandem.

Hap places reading glasses on his nose and leans close to the mantle. "She must've had 'em young." The long-tall Texan on the verge of retirement reaches for his notes. This is old hat for him. Once he reaches carpet, the fear of destroying valuable evidence underfoot subsides. He strolls around the sofa reciting his checklist of events.

"The call came in about 12:30. He's in shock, can't believe she'd do this. He says they're happy, just moved in two weeks ago. She's been busy with a decorator." Hap speaks without taking a breath, which leaves him resting against the bar panting. "We're trying to locate the decorator."

"Wait!" Squinting in the dim light, I focus on the occupants in the photos. Some of them look familiar. "Her name... what's her name?" I'm shaken by what I see.

Hap flips through the small spiral notebook. "Kacy Renea Flannery Wise, white female, 1-5 of 58." Hap reads from his notes again. "I guess there are a few others, but that's her maiden and present married names." He says with muffled laughter.

"She'd be better off dead." The voice echoes as nausea sets in. *No, no Megan—not here, not now.*

"Hell, they'd all be better off dead!" The unforgettable voice repeats in my head. Over and over again. And now... she is... dead.

"Her husband said he flew into DFW from... Houston at... 10:30. When she didn't answer the phone, he thought maybe she was already asleep." Distressed, he shuffles through the little pad again. "And get this." He doesn't look up from his scribbling. "He's 58 and she's 36." His eyes cut to me with a wink —our ages.

Strong coffee percolates in my gut. I grip the mantle for balance.

He fumbles for his notebook. As he turns the pages, they make a flapping noise. "He stays in Houston Tuesday and Wednesday nights, usually returns late on Thursdays, works for some oil company..." Hap scratches an eyebrow with the butt of his pen. "And he usually takes a cab home from the airport." The pad finds its way back in his blazer pocket. "The guy says no way this is suicide." After Hap speaks, he receives nothing verbal from Sam or me.

Absorbed in our normal routine, Sam continues his cursory observation of the room, determining what equipment we'll need to retrieve from the van. Hap chatters on.

"They haven't been married very long, about a year." No response from Sam or me. "We're trying to verify he was on that flight from Houston. He said she was in good spirits when he spoke to her this morn—I mean yesterday morning." He corrects himself, remembering it's already the next day. "Nothing earth-shattering going on in their lives."

The queasiness subsides. If I detach and remain silently objective, I can do this. *Come on Megan, just get through this. Then you can crawl into bed and forget it all.*

Things aren't always as they appear or as someone says they are, and Sam's twenty-five years of experience equips him with keen radar. I watch him zero in on seemingly inane items that indicate the husband's suspicions may be correct. An early lesson taught me a crime scene investigator should never draw conclusions from the obvious. I make mental notes of what to photograph. In a home this tidy, one thing out of place is cause for alarm, and I'll need to preserve it, at least on film.

"No forced entry. Looks pretty cut and dry," Hap says with a Texas twang even I can detect, and mine's almost as bad. "So what do ya think there, Sam?"

"Yeah, it *looks* that way."

"It looks to me like they had quite a life," I interject and proceed at a slow pace. My attention is drawn to cherub figurines and ornately decorated eggs perched on bookless shelves.

"Are there any pets?" My nose tells me no. A heavy scent of fresh paint and fruity potpourri stirs my stomach.

"No, no pets... and as you saw in the photos, the kids are

practically grown," Hap says, anticipating my next standard question. He wanders into the dining room and uses a knuckle to flip on the overhead light.

An older version of the familiar face in the photos sinks in. The nausea returns and my jaws tingle. Escape is all I can think, and the voice matching the face is all I hear. *"Better off dead!"* I have to get out before I throw up. I carefully retrace my steps to the door. Sam calls out. "Megan, where are you going?" Garbled words, to my ears.

The air outside gives me relief, but it's short lived. My head spins. *"Better off dead."* I brace myself with both hands on the brick exterior just in time to purge a fresh dose of nourishment for the newly planted Japanese boxwoods. As I recover, I notice a shoe print and a flattened cigarette butt between two of the bushes. Then tears, tears come soon after, much to my amazement. I knew Kacy. I'd known her many years ago, a whole lifetime ago. We'd met as young mothers, and I never liked her. Why was I shedding tears?

Did he mean it? Did he really want her dead? Does he want all of them dead, including me?

I'd hoped the immature decisions of my past would never enter my new life. The simple life I'd built for me and my boys. A past of foolish choices, letting my heart lead instead of my head, left my life in shambles. I can't let this place or thoughts of the past pull me back into the abyss I'd escaped so long ago. Unwelcome memories wash over me.

Still bent over, staring at the dark soil, I wonder if I should reveal my secret or feign continuing nausea. This is not the time for the two men I admire most in the world to learn of a past I'd put to rest long ago.

A heavy hand on the small of my back startles me and breaks my concentration. I wince as his other hand slowly creeps between my shoulder blades, rumpling my shirt. The foul stench at my feet prompts another brutal contraction—no need to lie. Hap leans over me, and I feel his knee at the back of my thigh.

Goose bumps swell with his touch on my now bare waist. I shiver from an inner chill in the predawn Texas heat.

"Are ya okay, girl?" I point to the footprint and cigarette butt. "I'll get it," Hap's low tone assures me.

Sam keeps his distance. He'd warned me in the early days I began working scenes with him, "I can handle the odor of everything but vomit. If you throw up anywhere near me, it'll make me want to vomit, so don't ever do it around me." I'd never tested his threat, but I had witnessed his participation at several crime scenes inundated with the putrid stench of decomposing remains. He worked diligently, without as much as a regurgitation burp.

"I think you should go on home and take care of yourself." Sam gestures a shooing wave from the doorway. "We can handle this, if Hap promises to stick around."

Hap cuts him short. "Oh, sure no problem, I got nothing better to do. Hey sweetheart, we'll get one of the patrol officers to run you home." Hap pulls me to an upright position. Cradling me in his armpit, I receive another sideways hug, the closest thing to sex we'll ever have. The smell of him comforts me. I fight the desire to bury my face in his chest and beg him to shield me from the recurring voice. *"They'd all be better off dead!"*

I don't think you're going to be 'better off' now, because she is dead. I manage not to give those words voice as I stare out the patrol car's window at the sparsely scattered tall brick houses. Their stoic mailboxes stand as sentinels in the dark to witness my final departure from this horrid place.

3

MONDAY, AUGUST 22, 1994, 8:00 A.M

I'm in the lab early. More than a week has passed since Kacy's death, and I've avoided Sam. Our secretary, MaryJo, asks me every morning if I'm okay. I snuck a peek at some of the scene photos, and it's definitely Kacy, Kurt's first wife. I need to tell Sam. He'll understand. I'll tell him very little. On one of a dozen trips between my office and lab bench, I spot an opportune moment. He's shooting the bull with the finger-print guys at the door to their office. Apparently, there's no pressing court time or administrative duties to distract him. I walk up behind him, and all eyes turn toward me.

"Well looky here boys, it's the A Team, together again! We hear tell y'all've been out on a few all-nighters!" Bob laughs loud, his belly shaking like Santa's as he attempts to diffuse the insinuation. I wrinkle my nose and throw him a sneer of disdain over Sam's shoulder.

There are three crime scene units for the county. Sam and I are part of the A unit. All units are responsible for major crimes such as homicides and suspicious deaths. The A unit consists of the chemistry section. We're also responsible for dismantling drug labs. We spend a lot of time in the field.

Clandestine laboratories in our part of the United States

mostly manufacture amphetamine and methamphetamine, known on the street as speed and crank. The use of chemists in the field is costly, but the safety benefit has proven invaluable.

Illegal drug labs are mazes constructed of intricate glassware full of pungent concoctions and electrical power supplies. To deconstruct the confusing labyrinth, knowledge of chemical reactions is vital. The process equates to dismantling a bomb. If the heat source is abruptly lost, the mixture of chemicals will cool too quickly and possibly explode. It may not take out a city block, but those close by would suffer. The sour odor of precursor chemicals such as phenyl acetic and formic acids combined with the sweet aroma of phenyl-2-propanone (P2P) permeates everything—a lingering stench Sam compares to the odor of sweat from a dead man's scrotum. It is worse than a decomposed body, but I never asked Sam how he concluded such. The unpleasant odors spare nothing, penetrating clothing, leather, and hair. We don Tyvek suits, gloves, and booties for protection. The heat and moisture generated by the body makes the work all the more unbearable. My first order of business after clandestine drug labs *and* decomps is to strip down in front of my washing machine and race to the shower.

The B unit consists of the fingerprint guys, Tom, Bob, and Ron. They resemble The Three Stooges and their simplistic names accurately reflect the level of intensity at which they work. Years spent hunched over desks, sedentary for hours, as they gaze into a magnifying glass at the whorls and bifurcations of latent prints. On scenes, they quicken their pace, whisking through, leaving black powder on every surface and little piles of crumpled tape underfoot.

Tom tells an old story about a fingerprint examiner observed for a couple of days by his coworkers in the same spot. No one realized he was dead. He always adds how, on the first day when they asked the guy to go to lunch, he grunted something they took for a no. Eventually gravity won, and as his weight and the wheels on his chair battled, he fell to the floor.

New technology transformed the three of them into less slothful, more productive tortoises. Our lab installed the only Automated Fingerprint Identification System (AFIS) in the region. It made the laborious task of identifying victims from the Branch Davidian Compound much easier.

Two evidence technicians and two serologists make up the C unit. They come out to assist with intense blood spatter in complex and/or multiple-victim scenes.

I wait for a lull in laughter. When it comes, I shake Sam's elbow. "Hey, can I talk to you, today... when you have time?" I bring way too much seriousness to the light mood I encountered. Everyone falls silent.

"Sure, now is good." He turns and takes off in the direction of his office without so much as a 'see ya later boys.' I follow.

With a detour to the break room, he retrieves a soda from the refrigerator. He enters his office, removes a heap of papers from an invitingly comfortable leather chair across from his desk, and motions for me to sit. The clutter in this room reminds me of an overgrown jungle. There are isolated stacks of evidence in progress, awaiting conclusive results. I keep him organized on the scenes we work, but this room is an impossible task. Sitting among the disorder on Sam's desk is a Diet Coke can another would assume empty, but I know it is at least one quarter full of leftover liquid and a minimum of six cigarette butts. Telltale ashes rest on top. On the computer desk behind him, two butts are perched on end and balance matching towers of ash. Stale nicotine and the blatant masculinity of this room takes me back to a place in time and a father I once knew.

Daddy called me "Magpie," his clever little bird. He nick-named each of his children, and with a gleam in his eye, he won my heart every time he said mine. I spent hours in his garage workshop watching him build and fix things. He'd prop his foot on a stool, and with a clink of his Zippo, smoke would swirl around his quandary.

"You see, Megan, when I put these two pieces like this, it

won't go back together." I learned to listen close, because he always set up the answer within the question. Holding the pieces up clearly at the wrong angle, seeming perplexed, he'd ask, "What's my clever little Magpie think we should do?"

"Daddy! Turn it this way—see it works now." I thought the smartest person in the world needed my seven-year-old help.

"Eureka! Magpie you've done it, and *here* is your reward." Magically, he would present me with a special trinket. Nothing girly—for me, a seashell, piece of pretty crystal, or an arrowhead was my prize. The ribbons, bracelets, and ornamental trinkets he gave to Tara. I secured my charms in a beautiful cherrywood box he made just for me. I've always kept the box under my bed. Every time I open it, the familiar clink and smell of the cigarette lighter propel me back to simpler days, and I caress *Magpie* carved on the lid.

My daddy left on the Christmas night before my ninth birthday. He didn't call or come see us for months at a time. Losing my grandparents to death was sad as a little girl, but my father's abandonment left me devastated and empty.

Sam became my mentor before I was out of college. I read about him several times in the *Star-Telegram*, reporters recounting his testimony in interesting murder cases. Sam would explain how the scientific evidence proved the accused was not telling the truth and bingo—guilty verdict.

One day I carried an article to a professor, curious how I could get into the forensic world with the chemistry degree I nearly had. He told me he would make some inquiries. Unbeknownst to me, the professor was an old colleague of Sam's. Before I knew it, I had an interview and was hired to work in the crime lab. I learned to process crime scenes and washed a lot of beakers. When I finished my bachelor's degree, he added drug analyses to my job duties with a hefty salary increase. I've been a firm believer in expressing your desires to others ever since. The professor is now a Tarrant County Judge.

Although he's a self-admitted slob, Sam's mess is organized. Funny how his profession is to make order from chaos, but in his own surroundings, he doesn't quite succeed. He'll get a wild hair every now and again and clean. Entropy habitually reoccurs.

Sam pushes back the clutter enough to find a pipe and leather tobacco pouch buried beneath. He loads the bowl and, using the blunt end of his fountain pen, packs the tobacco firm. The lighter's flame draws over the edge of the bowl as he inhales and puffs several times. The familiar routine produces billows of smoke and a sweet odor of vanilla.

The fix of nicotine allows him to rejoin my world. He looks at me over his reading glasses. "What's up?" He says in an upbeat tone.

The shuffled stack of Kacy's pictures fan under his elbow. "I know her," I spit out, expecting him to understand to whom I'm referring. No such luck. Oblivious, he places the pen and lighter in his breast pocket and puffs again.

"Who?" he asks with an uncertain defensiveness in his voice and a boyish grin. Perhaps wondering if I'm talking about someone with whom he's sure he'd been discreet.

"Her, the suicide victim." I point to the photos under his elbow. "She and I, well…" *Where do I start, or stop, how much do I tell him?* The whole story is more drawn out than a soap opera.

Don't try to tell him everything now, Megan. It's so complicated, bordering incestuous. He'll want to draw a relationship diagram, if he can find a blank sheet of paper.

"Our boys grew up together." There, that's good, a truthful beginning.

"Okay, I knew something was up. You've seen much worse and I haven't known you to lose it yet. That's not your style. You'd sooner swallow it than let any of these guys see a weakness in you. So tell me." As he speaks the words, I consider how he might judge me if he knew where my strength comes from. The reassurance in his voice is the signal of comfort I long for. I hope this will go no further.

"I was married a few years ago, to Glynn." I study his worn penny loafers under the desk.

"I know, and you have two sons, I know that too. Ian and…"

"And Connor," I fill in.

He circles an index finger in midair, indicating 'get on with it' and his growing impatience of my hesitance.

"I was married a second time… to Kurt." I look down at his shoes again. *Where are the pennies?*

Now I've said too much. His blank expression makes me nervous.

As Sam advised in my early days of testifying, "Use the K.I.S.S. method. Keep it simple, stupid, the jurors are regular everyday people, so explain what you did and how you did it in terms they understand."

Yeah, keep it simple, Megan, short and sweet.

I point to the photos again. "She was married to my second husband… before me."

Sam scrunches his eyebrows together, twists his head to one side, faces me, and spouts, "What?"

"Glynn introduced me to Kurt and Kacy when I was sixteen."

I think back to the very second I laid eyes on Kurt. An unrealized emptiness left me that day, reuniting souls from another time. I felt so drawn to him that it puzzled me for many years. Heartache returns with the memory.

"So your first and second husbands were friends? That's a new one on me." He cracks open the cold soda and taps the pipe on the edge of his metal trashcan.

"They were close as brothers at one time, yes." In personal matters, I'm not usually nervous around Sam, but this embarrassing segment of my life I'd rather not share.

Sometimes I get tongue-tied when it comes to seeking his direction on my work. I want to be sure I've covered all the bases before I bother him with instrumentation maintenance problems or analytical results I can't interpret or verbalize well. I should have organized the details of my past into a concise synopsis before presenting Sam with information he and Hap need to know. Sam possesses a Mensa-caliber IQ. He's smarter than everyone and, through underhanded compliments, often reminds his employees. As he contemplates the consequences of my confession, I stammer and decide to keep going.

"Well... Kurt and Kacy divorced a couple of years after I met them, and he married again."

"So he has—or had—two ex-wives? Uh, three, including you?"

"Yeah." I agree, knowing there's more but deciding to hold back what he would consider minutiae at this point.

"Where is Kurt now?"

"I wish I knew. He disappeared six years ago. Right after I started working for you. It's a long story, Sam, and those were some tough days. I won't bore you with it." Remembering as if it were yesterday, my left leg begins its nervous vibration. I wrap my arms around my waist and breathe deep to calm myself.

"You gotta give me something, Megan... I, actually wait, Hap needs to know all this. Or does he already?" Sam confirms he's aware Hap and I are close. "Does he know about Kurt?"

"No, he doesn't."

"Why did this guy leave? A man just doesn't walk away from his whole life for no reason. As much as some people would love to sometimes, they don't unless there's good reason."

"Kurt was a securities broker in oil and gas during our marriage. Apparently, he made some questionable deals. We got threatening phone calls. It was bad."

Sam's expression now says 'cut to the chase, Megan.'

"I guess before he disappeared, the Attorney General's office in Mississippi began investigating his brokerage for misappropriation of funds. Other states joined in, and by the time I heard about it, he was long gone. Anyway..." I rush to finish. "He left me. I don't know where he went or what happened to him. I wondered for a while if one of his investors hired someone to kill him. I've learned a lot more about his past since then, but I never found him." Raising a hand to my forehead, I lower my gaze to the floor again.

"I hoped I'd never have to tell anyone about all this. It's embarrassing. Especially you and Hap, I never wanted y'all to know." Looking up, I grow uncomfortable as he holds direct eye contact, in deep thought. I clench my still shaking knee.

"Stay away from this, Megan." Sam studies a photo of Kacy's suspended corpse, lights a cigarette, sips on his soda and continues. "Mr. Wise, her husband, doesn't think its suicide. Right now, I just don't know. We'll do everything we can to ease his suspicions. It's probably nothing, Megan, but just in case, you stay clear of it, okay?" He downplays my nervous admission with a wave of his hand, dismissing me from his presence.

"Okay." I stand to leave.

Then he expresses his true fear. "Damn! I hope he's not right. It'll ruin our perfect batting average!" I interpret his raised eyebrows as 'aren't we finished yet?'

Sam generally put things in perspective with baseball, and it tended to rub off on the rest of us. His boasting is warranted. We've not had an unsolved murder in years. Usually, it's just a matter of days before detectives have a good suspect we can tie to the crime. Recently, on a double homicide, the suspect left a thumbprint on the underside of a toilet seat and one of the fingerprint guys had the guy wrapped before we finished collecting evidence.

Sam takes great pride in being right. I haven't seen many cases stump him for long. He's one of the best in the country, sought by prosecutors as well as defense attorneys—in fact, everyone, from major multinational companies to the court-appointed attorneys, looking to give their client the best defense possible and the same quality of criminalists afforded to the state.

Sometimes, if the defense can get him first, they'll retain him so the state can't, even if his testimony won't help their case. Sam revels in this fact. We all do. We have a good team.

MaryJo speaks on the intercom. "Sam, line one."

He reaches for the phone. I pause in the doorway, unsure if I should tell him I'd already read the report and seen most of the pictures, including the ones I didn't take.

"Sam here." He runs fingers through his hair. "Aw, shit! I totally forgot!" He jumps up. "I'll be right there." Whipping his tie from lady justice's neck, he darts past me. *Guess not.*

"MaryJo, you didn't remind me," he says with a hint of anger and scurries down the hall.

She looks up as he blazes out the door. "Of what?"

We shrug in sync. I head back to the lab to get some work done.

The clock reads five straight up, and I'm glad this day is done. The last to leave, I lock the lab door and hear, "Hey little lady, hang on a second!" The dreaded country twang echoes down the hallway.

4

*I*t's Willie Ray Swackhaumer and his sidekick Leroy Banks from Springtown PD, with evidence to submit. I cringe. The thought of me alone with these two—*Oh, God!*

"Don't make us come back tomorrow. We drove as fast as we could to get here before five!" bellows Leroy.

"Yeah, I kept the pedal to the metal in Old Red." Willie Ray refers to his "classic" Corvette. The seventies must have been good to him because he seems stuck there.

"That's okay, come on in. What ya got?" I sigh and reluctantly hold the door open.

"Made a really big buy this mornin'. I need to know if it's good stuff or not cuz I'm suppose'd to buy more Wednesday." Leroy's slight lisp makes him sound like a baritone toddler.

"Okay Leroy, I'll do a quick color test." I take the envelope from him.

"Hey I told you! Call me Roy, not Leroy. I hate that damn name, makes me sound like a hick."

Laughing out loud, I think how true. Leroy, I mean Roy, grew up in Nocona, a small North Texas town. Springtown is the big city where he's the Mack Daddy of undercover cops. Actually, he's a big teddy bear of a man trying to look like a hard-ass biker with his beer belly, long hair, and earring.

Over the years, Willie Ray Swackhaumer shared far more about himself than I cared to know. For example, his German ancestors settled in the hill country in the 1860s and most people don't pronounce his name correctly, but he doesn't mind. During one such annoying encounter, he grabbed his crotch to emphasize why he prefers hammer to haumer.

He often grumbles that, if retirement pay could maintain his "playboy" lifestyle and child support for a couple more years, he'd chuck it all today for Mexican beaches. Tall and skinny, he wears his jet-black hair slicked back with more than 'a little dab' of Brylcreem. I swear he wears the same black leather vest, bolo tie, and Western-cut stretch pants every time I see him.

They follow me to the wet lab and watch closely as I lay out the apparatus for the presumptive testing. I place a small amount of the powdery substance in the well of a spot plate and, with a couple of drops of Marquis reagent, it fizzes and turns orange. Willie Ray's excitement spews. "Yep, that's crank all right, the good stuff."

I confirm the possibility its methamphetamine. Thinking I'll soon exceed their collective attention span, I explain the scientific reasons for the color change. "The orange color of the Marquis reagent tells us there's a primary amine present on the benzene ring. There are a few powders that could give us this, such as ephedrine, you know, like in the pills you take for a cold?"

Willie Ray inches closer to me and leans on my workbench, pretending interest. His chin rests on his palm. "Oh, yeah, I see."

I repeat the steps with another reagent. "And the blue color from the nitroprusside, or as it's labeled on your field kit, Simmons, is due to a secondary amine present on the ring."

Fifty percent success, I've lost Roy. He's trying to focus the stereo-microscope on his crusty cuticles.

"Ephedrine would also give us a blue color, but the response would be much slower." The odor from the Brylcreem invades my personal space.

Willie Ray's creepy devotion proves too much. "Of course, I'll need to do the instrumental analysis before I can issue a report or swear to anything in court." Satisfied with the results of their big buy, we head for the door.

Willie repeats his standard parting proposition. "Are you ready to handle me on the dance floor yet, little lady?" He holds his arms in a make-believe dance pose as he twirls on his heel. Roy hits the release bar of the heavy metal door with a thud, and a blinding light fills the narrow hallway.

"Oh, I'll never be able to keep up with you, Willie Ray. You're way to smooth for me." I shudder. The thought of dancing with this man is nauseating. "I'll see you boys later. Be good now and stay out of trouble."

At the far end of the parking lot, beyond the security fence, is an old blue pickup with a lone occupant in the driver's seat. Roy shuffles toward the car, oblivious.

"Well, now, how are we gonna have any fun if we stay out of trouble?" They walk toward Old Red. Roy slaps his thigh and laughs hysterically. A cloud of smoke billows from the tailpipe of the old truck. The two 'trained' officers don't seem to notice the pickup or perceive my sudden anxiety.

"Hey, hold up guys. Can you wait for me? Won't be a sec, let me grab my purse."

"Sure!" Willie Ray flashes a hopeful grin.

ON THE DRIVE HOME, I think of the photos. What isn't right? Why does her husband think it's not a suicide? Maybe it's the mark on the inside of her left thigh just above the knee. It *looks* like a cigarette burn. Kacy didn't smoke. Not during the years I'd known her. Matter of fact, she despised smokers. I didn't notice any ashtrays, cigarettes, or even a lighter anywhere in the house.

Maybe he saw the footwear impressions in the photos. Deep impressions in the sandy loam awaiting the pallets of sod were conspicuous. Sam's photo with oblique lighting didn't enhance tread pattern or show any noticeable individual characteristics. It looks like the leather sole of a boot. I could almost make out the Justin logo on the heel, which will be easy enough for Sam to determine.

My Ropers leave the same impression. I have a habit of noticing those things. My lipstick on a wine glass, fingerprints on the bathroom mirror, and the trail of my footprints on the beach.

Ahh, the beach. I can still feel the water loosening the sand beneath my toes and hear the hiss of the bubbles bursting as the emerald water retreated.

I attended the Florida State parent meeting a couple of weeks ago. As Ian settled in, I rented a car and drove through Apalachicola over the big bridge to St. George Island. The end of the summer season afforded me several days of judicious solitude at the Nautilus, where Kurt and I spent our honeymoon. The huge clapboard structure sits on the bay side of the island with its own dock. Otis Redding said it all.

Ian and I met on his second birthday. He reached to me and said, "Mama." He claimed me and melted my heart. His curious blue eyes spoke the words his old soul could not verbalize. In his short time on earth, he figured out early that life dealt him a dirty hand.

Now enrolled in college, my handsome athletic son confirmed my parental abilities. I change gears in my head as fast as I change them in my car.

While preparing a mental shopping list, I decide on pasta for dinner and salad with a vinaigrette dressing. Connor gets tired of pasta, but it's quick, low fat, and I love it. I'll go with bowtie and sundried tomatoes with mushrooms. I pull in the driveway and admire our home. The house and the boys were the really good things I held onto through two divorces.

After Kurt left, I sold every tangible asset in the house to pay my tuition and utilities. If I hadn't owned the house outright, I'm sure I would've lost it also. It was my divorce settlement from Glynn. A charming two-story brick with a large front southern porch, it's inviting and comfortable. I hope to spend the rest of my life here. I could never afford a mortgage on a house this size on my salary, but I do manage the upkeep, taxes, and insurance.

A couple of swallows from a glass of white Zinfandel ease the tension of the week. With water boiling, I make my way to the bedroom. The dogs follow my every step. I trade work clothes for shorts and t-shirt while listening to messages on the answering machine. I've ignored the flashing light for almost a week. After six increasingly frantic messages from my mother, the last one spouts a more demanding tactic. "Young lady! If I don't hear from you tonight, I'm sending one of your brothers over to check on you!"

We usually speak every other day, and I knew she'd be concerned, but I just couldn't face her, until now. I return to the kitchen, dialing her number on my new cordless phone.

"If only you knew what I've been through the last ten days." I tell her about Kacy's death. She comforts me as only my mother can.

"Well, Huunney!" The sympathy in her voice evaporates and she bristles with, "What if it's Kurt?"

"Mother!" She suspects him of everything from the bombing of post offices to the death of a housewife in Fort Worth. I assure her Kurt is a thief, not a killer.

My heart leaps when the front door slams. "Lucy, I'm home!" Connor, my anchor, announces with Ricky's Cuban accent. The familiar thud of his inline skates on the entry floor confirms his arrival.

"I just know one of these days he's going to crack the tile," I say aloud so she's aware of her grandson's entrance.

"Magpie, when you're fifteen, the world revolves around you and consideration is something others owe you. You were the same way, sweetie." I cast a disapproving glare in his direction as he walks into the kitchen. He mirrors my expression and adds a curl to his upper lip as he peers at the pot of boiling pasta.

Connor kisses my cheek, tips my wineglass for a sip. He listens to the conversation long enough to identify the person on the other end. Escaping a potential conversation, he exits yelling, "Hello, Granny!"

She shrieks, "Hi, Honey!" And without missing a beat, she's right back in our tête-à-tête. The way she overreacts exhausts me. "So why wouldn't he come back?"

"Kurt wouldn't risk coming back to this town—and why would he kill her? They've been divorced fifteen years!" I try to ease her fears.

After a long pause, she gives her standard response for all these conversations. "I don't know, but I wouldn't put it past him, the son-of-a-bitch! I wish they'd catch him and string him up by his balls, so you could put all of this behind you. Megan, why do you keep hanging onto your past with him like it was so wonderful?" She huffs. "He left you with a mountain of debt and not so much as a kiss my ass!"

"Mother!" I cut her off before she can remind me, again, how I had to file bankruptcy because of all the debt he left me.

IT SEEMS my attempt at a normal life was destined for failure long before I got swept up in the disastrous wake of Kurt Terrell. Perhaps a genetic thread granted a providence of my birthright —emotional and physical abandonment. The sequence started long before me, with my mother, Katherine Raigene.

She never was quiet or demure. 'Katy Ray' exploded from the womb into the arms of reverent and repressed Southern Baptist parents. My favorite photograph of her, as a small child, has her dressed in frilly lace, with eyes like mine, dark and serious. Chubby cheeks frame a defiant smile straining to mask a tortured expression of discomfort. Her mirror opposite sits beside her, a petite, blue-eyed blonde girl with a sweet smile. With my Aunt Yonnie, Granny would say she got her doll. "Katy Ray! Why can't you be more like Tonya?"

As a teenager, Katy Ray discovered her father's deep prejudices toward the "Negros" and began a lifelong fight for civil rights. Although her efforts did little to sway Fort Worth in the late 1950s, she remained vigilant. She joined a small group in Dallas, protesting any event with racial undertones, especially if the newspapers or TV cameras were present.

I like to think she made a difference; she talks as if she did. I do hear regret when she tells of the police and protester altercations. I hear reluctance and fear in the grandiose stories. Maybe she merely embarrassed her parents and further alienated her mother.

She met my father at a rally for civil rights in Wichita, Kansas. He was a poor sharecropper's son on a mission to bring attention to the poverty plaguing Oklahoma and Kansas twenty years after the Dust Bowl left them in ruins. William "Billy" Brooks, a stunningly handsome young man with a thick mop of red hair, had an eye for the ladies. He served in the Air Force as navigator on a B-36 Peacemaker, on leave when they met. Stationed at Carswell Air Force Base in west Fort Worth, he had no desire to farm the vast Kansas cornfields like his ancestors. All I remember of the farm is running through tall corn on a summer day and the horrific experience of peeing in an outhouse.

My parents stayed married through four live births and a stillborn. I think the death of a child drove them apart. I can't fathom the loss they felt. My mother gained weight with each pregnancy, and Billy Brooks' wandering ways resurfaced.

Mom raised her children alone, doggedly determined to make it on her own, never asking her parents for help, unless the food ran out. I know now she wanted us to experience the happiness a modest life offers without the weight of expensive trappings. She hoped if we learned to appreciate a basic existence, we'd be better equipped to survive the difficult days most certain to come. Her fight to right the entire world of injustice whittled down to four impressionable children.

Before that first summer arrived, our house became the hangout of the local hippies as she grasped at the youth she'd forsaken for family. Some days, we'd pile into Moody Blue, our 1964 midnight blue convertible Chevy Impala, and drive the country roads to Mustang Park on the south shore of Benbrook Lake. Teenage girls placed garlands of wild flowers on our heads, and we'd chase each other through circles of people passing around funny-smelling cigarettes.

Mom supported our family of five as a seamstress for Handley's Dry Cleaning and Alterations. On weekends and evenings, she designed and created costumes for Casa Mañana Theatre and go-go dancers in the area clubs. At least that's what she told her children. The girls were actually strippers, dancing in the local gentlemen's establishments. My sister and I wrapped ourselves in the long fringe and sequin-covered fabrics of the dancers' outfits. Our little brothers giggled as we danced to *"Break on Through to The Other Side"* and pretended we were the go-go dancers on *Laugh-In*. We said "far out" and "groovy" and pulled two fingers over our eyes like Batman did when he danced.

We were a strange, inseparable little family—Tara, me, James, and Edward, stair-stepped with two years between. At bedtime, Tara read to us from *The Boxcar Children* series. We pretended the adventures of James, Jessie, Violet, and Benny were ours, trying to escape the wicked clutches of their mean old grandfather.

～

"I REALLY THINK we should change the subject now, okay? We've been over this more times than I care to remember." We talk about how she wishes one of my brothers would give her another grandchild, since my sister won't.

"Geeze, Mother, lighten up on Tara. She's a thirty-eight-year-old lesbian who's never expressed a desire for children. And believe me, after my history with men…"

She cuts me off with a laugh. "Don't go there Megan, don't even say it."

"You started it. Hey I need to let ya go and finish making dinner, okay? I love you."

"I love you, too. Call your Mother sometimes, will 'ya?"

Tara surprised us with her lesbian confession during Thanksgiving dinner three years ago. She retreated to Dallas to live in a more welcoming community. Try as she might, my mother isn't handling it well. But she *did* raise us to be independent freethinkers. Tara helps run the AIDS clinic in the gayborhood.

I hang up with an exaggerated, "Okay, I *am* sorry I haven't called. I'm sure you understand, with all I've been going through at work. Bye, love you." Click.

Connor and I eat dinner in front of the TV with *Murphy Brown* and *Northern Exposure*. Since Ian left, this is our routine. He's only been gone for a couple of weeks, and the family he left is unconventional, again.

Me, my son, and our rescue dogs are what's left of the family. Someone dumped the Keeshond pups infested with ticks, fleas, and worms in our local park. We shortly discovered we misnamed them, as Beta became her brother's dominate. Nursing them to health provided a distraction and a common goal of compassion after Kurt left us.

I rotate the laundry once more, fold dry clothes, pour another glass of wine, and give my man-sized child a kiss on the forehead. He echoes goodnight, and I seek the refuge of my bed. Thoughts of the past remind me how uncomplicated and 'traditional' life used to be: Kurt, Kacy, Glynn, me, and all our boys having dinner and playing cards. Playing house, really—we were *too* young for babies and bills.

As the result of a high school love, Glynn, at 21, was already a father when I met him. Ruby, Glynn's mother, laid claim to Ian before his first breath.

After high-priced attorneys trashed the young girl, she relinquished all parental rights. Glynn's family money and 'ruthless Ruby' persevered. She planned to raise the boy herself until I showed up. My appearance threw a curve at her second chance of motherhood.

Ruby Mae Dalrymple set out to sabotage my relationship with her son. Her afternoon bridge club members sipped sherry and conspired. From the wrong side of the tracks and with no formal upbringing, I was not worthy of a Dalrymple. Glynn persisted through the rumors to defy his mother and claim me as his bride. Successfully courted, we married months before my eighteenth birthday.

Truth was, Ruby grew up as poor as me. She saw herself in Ian's mother, pregnant by a rich man's son, married at the end of a shotgun. "Her" money had an interesting tale of its own. Back in 1930, Glynn's paternal grandfather worked for Columbus Marion "Dad" Joiner on the Daisy Bradford oil rig in east Texas. Tired of drilling dry holes, many men were ready to quit and go home to their families. Dad, ever the charmer, talked some into staying by upping percentages of the profit. A few days later, they hit the biggest oil reserve in the world, the Black Giant. Glynn's grandfather became extremely wealthy overnight.

Looking back, I am not sure if I fell in love with Glynn or the idea of a real family. My parents' divorce when I was young and my mother's difficulty raising us alone was far from the *Leave it to Beaver* life I wanted. I promised, if she'd let me get married, I'd start college in the fall. I didn't. On my nineteenth birthday, I discovered I was pregnant with Connor. While my high school friends attended frat parties and traveled to Europe, I was potty-training and fighting stretch marks. Losing touch with my friends left me more isolated and dependent on Glynn. I worked evenings as a cashier at the neighborhood supermarket. After

Connor's second birthday, I secretly searched for scholarship money and planned to go to college. I asked Kurt to help me tell my husband. Glynn was angry. He wanted his codependent wife home, taking care of him. I wasn't happy, and I didn't want to be unhappy forever.

I started college, and the disintegration of our marriage accelerated. Exposure to academia expanded my world far beyond Glynn.

"And the hypotenuse is the sum of the squares of both sides of the triangle. It's called the Pythagorean Theorem." Merely helping Ian with geometry homework was taken as an insult to his intelligence.

Glynn's suspicious nature dwindled my time with friends to an occasional invitation to 'girls' night out,' which he'd agree to only if he came along. Kurt was my only confidant. My marriage was a sham, but the rest of the world didn't have to know. I kept up the façade with my family and classmates, but Kurt knew.

Kurt encouraged. "You deserve a good man. You don't have to put up with his drinking."

His interest in my new world was flattering. The attraction I felt for him, even in my husband's presence, was almost painful. I rejected any notion he could possibly feel the same.

As Glynn's drinking became intolerable, keeping a happy face in the midst of denial was easier than the reality of his threats.

"Go ahead and leave. You'll never see Ian again. I guarantee you that!" I had no legal rights to the boy I raised.

A school counselor suggested I attend Al-Anon meetings. I repeated Einstein's definition of insanity—you can't expect things to change if you keep doing the same thing over and over again. It was up to me.

Finally, I changed, for myself and my sons. I changed the locks, I changed the bedsheets, I packed Glynn's bags and changed his address. He'd have to fight me for every inch, including Ian. Possession is nine tenths of the law in Texas.

The divorce started nasty. Fortunately, Ruby grew too feeble to battle for Ian. Glynn reluctantly granted me the house, custody of Conner and guardianship of Ian with child support for both. Financial aid helped me attended Women's University of Texas. Part-time jobs as a lab assistant and tutor provided enough to make it, without much left for extras. Devoid of Glynn's drunken rages, we thrived in our home of virtual silence.

School and working on campus in Denton meant more time away from home for me. Ian, nine, and Connor, six, spent my time away with their grandmothers. My worries about their adjustment to the stress were allayed. Between grandmothers, the boys wanted for nothing. Ruby's verbal condescension flourished, but in the solitude of home and hearth, life was on a steady keel.

As for Glynn, child support was a small price for the relief of his parental responsibility. Being a legit free agent appeared to outweigh the loss. He bought a black Trans Am with a gold bird on the hood and spent his days playing golf.

I spent long hours struggling in the chemistry labs, forced to steal time away from cleaning and cooking to spend with my sons, and it was the only time I didn't feel guilty for not studying. I was moving forward. I was living again, not merely sustaining a stagnant life.

Kurt and his second wife, Missy, divorced the year before Glynn and I split. He didn't pounce all at once, yet he was always there. Wandering unconnected to anything or anyone, so lost, I welcomed him into my empty heart and finally my bed.

THE MEMORIES UPSET ME. It's going to be a restless night. I fall asleep to David Letterman. Loud predawn commercials wake me with a start. Beta jumped, knocking the remote to the floor, just out of my reach. Stretching for it, I tumble to the floor. Under the bed beyond the remote, I spot the treasure box I've kept hidden there for so long. The desire to re-inventory the old and newly acquired contents pales in comparison to the promise of a little more sleep. The strange key I recently added to the box still remains a mystery to me. I'll let it be, for now.

5

WEDNESDAY, OCTOBER 19, 1994

*I*t's a hectic week. Several coworkers are in Steamboat Springs for the forensic scientists' conference held every fall. The bulk of this year's conference is on drug analysis. I prefer the gory crime scene workshops to the tedious and boring lectures on spectroscopy and chromatography methods.

Lucky for me, Sam approved my request to attend a joint meeting next month of regional forensic scientists and international crime scene reconstructionists in the only city that comes close to Fort Worth on the humdrum scale, Oklahoma City.

The intake of evidence and juggling questions from baby DAs who haven't taken the time to read the new drug laws has robbed me of valuable alone time in the lab. When MaryJo finally shows up to work, I head to the lab to salvage the rest of the morning.

Being alone in the lab is great. I crank up some tunes and plan to make a to-do list as soon as I sit down at my desk. I'll need to make arrangements for Connor to stay with his dad and step-mom and someone to come feed the dogs. The list is never written. My mind drifts from one thought to the next as I remove my evidence bin from the vault and start the familiar routine.

I envy Sam. His only responsibility is to his job. Shortly after his wife died, he sent his only child, a daughter, to boarding school in France, as instructed in the trust fund left to her. If he has much more of a personal life, he never lets anyone know. Rumor has it he's boinking MaryJo, but nobody really cares. Although it seems he has no close friends, he and Hap drink together from time to time. Ritual male bonding toasted on occasion with a bottle of Glenfiddich, kept in a drawer at Sam's knee.

In the middle of presumptive tests for psilocin in a mushroom case, MaryJo pages me. "Megan, line one."

"Hey, Babe!" The smooth deep voice of a late-night disc jockey belongs to Assistant District Attorney Tyler Carson. "What's goin' on? How many bad guys are ya puttin' away today?" I haven't heard from him in weeks, since our last sweaty encounter.

With mixed emotion, I reply. "Are you asking about anybody in particular?" Trying to remember whether psilocin or psilocybin will deteriorate at a high-temperature gas chromatography run had my thoughts far from the unexpected call.

My businesslike tone slows his response. "Did I catch you at a bad time?"

"No, just the usual hell around here. I'm glad you called." I jot down the result of the "fast blue" color change, set the test tube rack to the side, and give Tyler my full attention.

"Well, I won't keep you, but I had an idea. How 'bout we go to the races in Shreveport this weekend, get away from everything, just you, me, and a dozen horses?"

I'm surprised at his invitation. We've never spent more than a few hours together. A whole weekend might be a little too much. It's not a good idea, and I stumble for the proper reply.

"Well…" Mentally running through my social calendar, I remember Connor's going to his dad's after school today. He won't be home until Sunday, but with a skeleton crew, I can't leave town. There's always a chance we'll get called to a scene.

"Plan on Friday after work. I'll call you tonight with the details."

"No, sorry I can't... it's just me this weekend. I'm on call. If we have a major crime scene, I have to be here. Here's an idea." I glance around the corner to make sure no one can hear me. "Why don't you come over tonight, for dinner?"

"Okay sure. I've got something to take care of first, shouldn't last more than an hour. How about 7:30?" Tyler's patterned response. He'll give me time, but it's always going to be after something more pressing. This leaves me feeling I'll never be pretty enough, smart enough... not good enough. Something's always more important than me, or perhaps it's his subconscious retaliation for my reservations early in our relationship.

"Sure." What else could I say?

"Okay, it's a date. Gotta run, see ya tonight." Click.

I stare at the receiver, the dial tone humming. I hang it back on the wall under the clock. I'll have to hurry and get the fungi extraction set up for the night before I leave. There's so much to do, and if Tyler is on time, it'll be a close call. What to make for dinner? Something... with mushrooms.

TYLER and I met a couple of years ago at the courthouse. I testified about my laboratory results on the first drug case he prosecuted. He asked me out for drinks to celebrate his first felony conviction. I took advantage of the opportunity to place him in uncomfortable surroundings and question him, as he had me, on the witness stand earlier. I chose the White Elephant Saloon, a honky-tonk in the Stockyards.

"Mr. Carson, I detect by the lack of accent you're not from 'round these parts. Where do y'all hail from?" With my best Southern Belle, eyelash-fluttering drawl, I added, "And, sir, how is it you came to be a lawyer?"

Much to my surprise, his response came in rhotic Jersey

tongue. "Raymond Burr... all the kids on my block would watch Scooby Doo afterschool... I'd wacth old reruns of Perry Mason... no shit."

We laughed. "No shit? Sooo, you're from New Jersey?"

"Yeh, no shit! New-wawk, New Jerw-see." He slumped in the chair and took a long drag from the cigarette pinched between his thumb and middle finger.

"How'd you end up here, in Fort Worth?"

Musicians took the stage, twisted tuning pegs and plucked strings. The lead singer shot me the same look of disapproval I'd received from the bartender. I knew a white woman sitting in a country bar with a black man probably wouldn't garner much approval. The pioneering spirit of my female ancestors failed me. The band confirmed my uneasiness, opening with the prophetic *Crime of the Century*. Defensive lyrics recalled the killing of a man ... "really wasn't my idea. I have to live with it for the rest of my life." The singer didn't sound very sorry.

Tyler scooted a few inches closer, blocking my view of the band. "Oh, this is not the end. This is just a stepping stone to achieve the higher goal. When I graduated from SMU, I heard Tarrant County DA's office was hiring, and it beat going back to New Jersey." Tyler didn't appear the least bit uncomfortable in the deepest belly of Cowtown. I wondered if he even noticed the dissention, or was he used to it?

He described his journey from the finest private school in the northeast to a college football scholarship and how a dream-crushing injury led to law school instead.

"And besides, I like Texas. The weather's not so bad and the women are... well, not so bad either," he said with an exaggerated nasal twang as he reached for my hand.

"Gee, thanks." Leaning back in the chair, I crossed my arms. "What's the higher goal?"

He told me of his parents' plan for him to follow in his father's footsteps to someday take his place on the bench as a federal judge in the 2nd Circuit District Court.

"Wow! Your Dad's a Federal Court Judge?"

"Oh yeah, mean Judge Carson. Remember that old TV show when they'd say, 'Here come da Judge. Here come da Judge'?"

"Flip Wilson, I think it was the Flip Wilson show." I scratched my temple and felt flush.

"He was talkin' about my father!"

I sat back and studied his claim. "You're kidding!"

"No I'm not. Flip Wilson was very proud of my dad. They grew up together."

"My parents' mission in life was to remove all racial barriers. They sent me to private schools." He emphasized "remove all racial barriers" with a baritone vibrato.

Tyler grinned. "I was the only black kid in that school."

We ordered more drinks. Mesmerized with his voice, I propped my chin on a palm, engrossed in our conversation. The lyrics dissolved and the tense mood of the room liquefied.

"I was a straight-A student with perfect attendance." Although he was smart, athletic, and everyone's friend as a child, he shared with me how he felt painfully alone in a world where those traits were discounted by the one obstacle his parents couldn't remove—the color of his skin.

He admitted he'd never shared his story with anyone before me. I asked why. Melancholic, he replied, "No one ever asked."

Empathy went unspoken. Desegregation graced our school with the adorable lone black child, LaDonna Dillon. I never truly understood her pain. Being more than average wasn't an option. She dumbed down her smarts and became our clown. If she let her guard down for a second, she'd have been eaten alive. Most days, I was a helpless bystander, afraid of being called a nigger lover and walking home with broken glasses again.

Tyler hesitantly revealed the cards he kept so close to his chest and a little of what made him tick. Once exposed, the fragile foundation of his success contrasted his youthful innocence and piqued fascination within me.

I wanted to rise from spectator status, accept the challenge and invite more, much more. Our first dates felt taboo and reckless as our friendship became a relationship. We connected on a physical and mental level. He was all mine, all the time, for a while. The insurmountable reservations of racial disparity blocked a progression beyond the privacy of the bedroom. Then one day, a less self-conscious, smarter, prettier blonde caught his attention.

Forward-thinking metropolitan cities were accepting of mixed-race couples. Fort Worth was still sporting a century-old bruise while struggling to crawl out of the sixties and, although my mother would think my dating a black man avant-garde, I knew Sam and Hap would not.

Now, I watch women come and go in Tyler's life. I'm not sure why, but he always returns to me. He romanticizes I'm his foothold, an anchor to right himself after battling rough waters. I fear the driving force of our relationship is fueled by an intense sexual attraction and a base understanding to expect nothing more than friendship in public. We may never regain the virgin passion of those first exciting days, and it's my fault. I want to reconnect at the level we once shared.

EIGHT O'CLOCK, right on time for Tyler, he saunters in with the latest Denzel Washington video in hand. He's commented in the past of his resemblance to the actor. Other than the overall proportion, I don't see it. I guess it's not so much what others think, but what you think of yourself. Tyler's ability to maintain the athletic physique of high school and college football days makes up for the lack of Denzel's polished bravado. I can't speak for the women in the movie star's life, but Tyler's added ability to maintain my satisfaction surpasses anything I've seen on the big screen from Denzel.

If I hadn't pushed Tyler away, maybe we could've had more —if I'd silenced the inner voice of condemnation and pushed through fear to intimacy. If I weren't so broken, I could venture past the realm of sweaty sex and detachment. I'm not fixable.

I was a fool to trust Kurt, a fool to give so much. He ripped open old wounds when he left me. An unheeded lesson I learned in my ninth year—love is the only real power. No one will ever control my heart again. I'm done playing nice, innocent and vulnerable.

6

*O*ur hellos are muffled by the growling and barking of the dogs. I put them outside and return to find outstretched arms pleading me to fill the void between them. With a tiptoed kiss we embrace and he lifts me. Our descent to the floor is accompanied by one waywardly tossed garment after another landing about the room. Primal urgency forces exploring hands and mouths to probe for salty soft places. Pinned under his weight, I push against the firm smooth chest. The stark contrast of my white hand against his sienna skin is the visible reminder of my deep Southern roots. I drink in my secret. Perhaps it strengthens our attraction for each other. He licks and playfully nips my breasts, then follows an invisible trail parting my thighs. I begin a journey to the place few men have taken me. He'll give me what I want, but I know Tyler can't give me what I need. I reach orgasm and beg for more. He backs away and chuckles softly.

"This is just the appetizer baby, dessert will be served… " He licks his fingers, "… after dinner."

"Ahh, no you can't stop now!" The coarse texture of the Berber carpet embosses my palms as I rise from the floor. He helps me to my feet, and my gelatin legs wobble. He smacks my butt.

"What's this on your back?" His fingers reach raw skin covering the vertebra between my shoulder blades.

"Ow!" I jerk away and teasingly respond, "Painful pleasure has no measure."

He fiddles around with the VCR while I dish up Chicken Marsala with plenty of mushrooms and pour the wine. I feel all tingly as the wine warms my naked body. We settle in front of the TV as the movie starts. Tyler attacks his dinner with the same gusto he devoured me earlier. Seal plays softly in the background as we partake of dessert and fall asleep. The phone rings at 1:00 a.m. It's either Sam or a family emergency. I'm glad it's Sam. I rush out the door and leave Tyler curled up in the goose-down comforter, a barrier against the air conditioning set just above freezing after our sensuous, sweaty encounter.

I drive to the address scribbled on a loser lottery ticket. The thought of possessing an afterglow brings a smile. Gravel flies and crunches as I speed down the secluded lane toward the police lights pulsating against the tin siding of the lone trailer.

Hap approaches my car. "Did we interrupt something?" He raises his eyebrows and his swarthy words confirm my suspicion that he'd notice the blush in my cheeks. *I wonder if he fantasizes about me.*

I display a devilish grin and push him back with the car door. "So, what we got?"

"It's a run–of-the-mill domestic. Husband beat his wife with something. We don't have a weapon yet. She's been Careflighted. Doesn't look like she's gonna make it, but she's hangin' on, for now. The husband did it, but he's feedin' us a big line of bullshit."

I jot down the particulars, case number, names, and DOB's in my notebook, grab a flashlight and head to the trailer. The officer keeping the scene log takes my name, and I duck under the barrier tape.

Sam's at the bottom of the steps, waiting. "This one's yours. You take the lead and tell me what we're gonna need."

My gut clenches. I know I can do this, but for Sam to feel I'm ready to lead a scene investigation will be nerve-racking under his watch. Climbing the rickety wooden steps doesn't help. We enter another trashed household.

A bloody mess within five feet of the front door marks the spot of her final attempt at freedom from this hell. Still, musty air suspends the odor of fresh blood. Surrounding the major pool of blood lay the scattered remnants of EMT trash, articles opened in haste to save her life. Piles of clothing on soiled carpet and stacks of dirty dishes in the kitchen sink verify my theory of trailer trash.

Every scene feels new to me, each provides an opportunity to hone a method of preserving and documenting evidence combined with the potential to learn a new one. A person's life that has ended so abruptly is such an open book. Unfinished tasks, such as the partial grocery list on the kitchen counter or laundry left to fold on the sofa, remind me of my own chores in need of completion. This place purely disgusts me. I can't let my prejudices keep me from finding a redeeming quality in this woman's life to do the best job I can.

Blood spatter trails on the ceiling and walls are directional, indicative of cast-off from numerous blows, but the blood absorbed in the carpet is hard to distinguish from the myriad of stains.

Sam mumbles something unintelligible.

"What?" I holler from a back room where a newly purchased ironing board rests against the closed closet door. The board I bought a few days ago is already in service. Perhaps she intended to improve this place and her life, but never got the chance. There, I found a redeeming quality. I make my way back to the hall.

"I said this doesn't look like a virgin scene—this isn't the first beating that's happened here." He shines his flashlight on the floor and nudges a broken toy aside with his foot.

Even in this mess, detachment grows increasingly difficult. I see the same brand of toilet tissue, toothpaste, and ketchup I buy. It affects me to discover, aside from the lack of housekeeping skills, this victim is not much different than me.

I turn to Sam. "This is going to take a while, and looks like we'll need to get the woo juice."

Hap pokes his head in the door. "She's dead. Hernandez just called from the hospital. I guess he got a statement before she died, said her husband did it."

WOO JUICE IS LUMINOL, our safety net. It develops latent blood stains, the invisible clues left undetected just a decade ago. My first experience with Luminol was at the homicide scene of a prominent businessman. There were no visible bloodstains on the beige carpet anywhere in the house except in the bedroom where the murder took place. Someone tracked through the large pool of blood, but appeared to stay in close proximity to the body.

Sam decided, after we finished collecting evidence and processing for fingerprints, to use the new technique. "What the heck, let's see what happens." As I sprayed the Luminol, footprints lit up and Sam marked them with a Sharpie. A glowing occurs because of the reaction between the Luminol and the iron in the hemoglobin of blood. This reaction is referred to as chemiluminescence. It also occurs with other metals, but is most intense with iron.

As we went through the house, the now visible left footprints led us to the phone in the kitchen, down every other stair to the basement garage, to a shelf containing cans of spray paint. Then the small footprints retraced their entire route back to the bedroom where the estranged wife sprayed the macabre message "1 down 3 to go BITCH" in an attempt to cast suspicion away from herself. With every new revelation, an entourage comprised of a Texas Ranger, Hap, and two patrol officers followed us through the darkened house. Their oohs and aahs lead us to start calling Luminol 'woo juice'. The glowing petite footprints betrayed her.

DURING THE CURSORY search of the living room and kitchen area, it doesn't take Sam long to locate the murder weapon. With his flashlight beam, he follows a trail of blood drops on the kitchen floor to the refrigerator. He shines the light between the refrigerator and the wall.

"Well, look what we have here." There, propped in the corner beside the broom and mop that have never seen a hard day's work, is a wooden baseball bat.

Sam backs away. "You start the photos and I'll get out of your way."

When he turns to make his way past me and miss a chair, he accidentally bumps a plastic cup perched on the counter. His reaction is much quicker than I would have guessed. He catches it in midair without losing a drop of the moldy concoction inside. We just look at each other with relief.

"Whew!" he breathes. "I'll get the rest of the equipment."

I take my overall photos, strategically place the evidence markers and photograph again. I wonder why this woman allowed her life to get so out of control.

My experience has taught me this is one of only two endings to a cycle of abuse. Escape is the only alternative to this nightmare.

At 3:00 p.m., finally home, I go through the routine of checking my mail, phone messages, and let the dogs in. Thunder cracks and the sky finally opens. Completely exhausted from the long day, I look forward to spending the rest of it sleeping alone. Tyler left long ago.

THURSDAY, October 20, 1994, 10:00 p.m.

12:42 flashes on my alarm clock. Hard rain provided the perfect environment for deep sleep. The air is thick with humidity. All I know of the time is the electricity went out the last time forty-two minutes ago. The ringing phone jars consciousness to my brain.

7

*G*od—I just went to sleep. Sam sounds as though he shares my thoughts. At least this time it's on my side of town. He's calling from the lab. He's already restocked the van with the items we used only hours ago. I start to write a note to Connor, then remember he's with his dad.

For coffee, I stop at the Kwick Sack. I hold my insulated cup under the dripping black stream to capture the first full, strong cup. I don't have the time or patience to wait for a full pot.

"What'd ya think of that storm? We sure needed the rain," Tammy hollers over the columns of chips and cookies blocking my view of her.

"I slept right through it." I stand on one leg then shift my weight to the other.

"Where you headed tonight, Megan?" I brief the apple-bodied late-night clerk cautiously. The location is so close she may actually know the victim.

I toss a dollar bill on the counter and update her on what's happened since our last similar encounter. "You put that away. You're a public servant just like the police, and ya never see one of them around here this time of night." She waves her outstretched arm at the expansive glass storefront.

"Ya know Megan, if you'd just call before you leave the house, I'd start a fresh pot for ya. It would be sittin' here waitin' for ya."

"Tammy, sometimes I hardly find two matching shoes before I get out of the house. Maybe I'll remember next time." Checking out my shoes, I stuff the dollar in my pocket and head for the door.

She loves the break in monotony as much as me. I'm sure she makes a good wife and mother for her high-school sweetheart husband and towheaded brood. "You drive careful, hun," she says as I push the door open. "I'll be praying for the family." Sweet Tammy, one would never know from her looks her faith is so strong. With over-dyed blonde hair and a raspy cough from far too many cigarettes, she looks more like a biker chick than a church lady. Several nights, when I was so tired I could hardly walk and was barely awake, she would place her hands on mine and channel 'God's power and strength' into me. She doesn't know I don't really believe in the power of prayer, but I have to admit, it always helps to know someone cares. I play along.

Finally on the road, I swerve from lane to lane and balance my cup of coffee too big for my drink holder and too hot for me to hold. Just a few sips of the concoction bring me to an alert state. I curse the standard-shift Honda Accord bought many years ago. I hope I'm not pulled over. Sure, I can always get out of it with a flash of my badge and a quick explanation about where I'm headed. It would slow me down, though, and I have to get to the scene before Sam is tapping his fingers.

The house is in a decent neighborhood with good-size brick tract homes, small yards, and alleys. White Settlement is a middle-class city cupped by Fort Worth from east to west and bordered to the north by General Dynamics, Carswell Air Force Base, and Lake Worth beyond. Not many serious crimes happen here. I live just to the west—five minutes away. I get out of my car and walk up the alley. I don't see the van or Sam. Barrier tape is strung from a fencepost on one side of the house across the alley to a neighbor's tree. The garage door on the left is open. Hap pulls up with a woman I don't recognize. They approach me.

"Long time no see," Hap says sarcastically. "Yeah, sure could use some more coffee 'bout now."

I down my last sip. "Who's this?" I point to the dark-haired woman with him.

"Oh yeah. Megan, this is Jackie Taylor. She just transferred into our unit from economic crimes."

I offer my hand. "Nice to meet ya. How do ya like it so far?"

"This is a change, but I think I'll like it just fine," Jackie says as we shake hands.

Two uniformed officers walk toward us. "Looks like suicide to me," one of the officers says. They relate what they saw and reassure each other as to the assumption of suicide. The estimation on how long she has been dead based on their limited knowledge of rigor and lividity is speculative at best.

I turn to Jackie and whisper. "Remember they're patrol with very little crime-scene experience." She nods her head and smiles.

Sam joins us without being noticed. He looks at Jackie, sizing her up, and then looks at Hap, waiting for an introduction. Hap is oblivious to Sam's insinuation.

"Well, since Hap won't introduce us…"

"Oh Sam, I'm sorry." I touch his arm. "This is Jackie Taylor. She's working with Hap now. She came from… where was it again?"

Sam grabs Jackie's small hand and shakes eagerly, catching her off guard. "Uh, economic crimes—nothing as exciting as this!" Jackie brandishes a Miss America smile, politely places her left hand on top of his right and stops the shaking.

"S… S… Samuel Miller," he stutters with a hiss.

"It's a pleasure to meet you, Mr. Miller, you're a legend. Well, I mean I've heard so much about you."

"It's okay, I get that all the time, and please call me Sam. Mr. Miller was my father." Flattery becomes him.

Sam's close proximity to her makes me notice her petite frame in contrast to his. Jackie's long, dark hair is pulled back loosely at the nape of her neck. Tendrils float in the breeze, and she keeps brushing them out of her violet eyes. Her striking beauty tells me she must be much younger than me. I wonder if perhaps her fast rise from junior detective to homicide is because promoting a female would keep the minority numbers up to acceptable affirmative action standards.

Sam and I walk around a brand-new Dodge Ram pick-up through the open garage door. The door on the right is closed. Hap's boots scrape on the concrete as he joins us.

"Seems her boys caught a ride home from school when she didn't show to pick 'em up. They went in the front door with a key, grabbed a snack, and watched TV until the husband came home, about 9:30. He comes and goes through the back gate." He points to the big maroon truck. "That's his truck there. He thought she was at work, until he listened to the messages on the machine. Her work called a couple of times, wondering where she was. They needed someone to cover her shift at the hospital. She's a nurse at Cook's, four 'til two? The boys told their dad she never showed at school, and that's when he found her... here." Hap lifts his Bic pen to the tiny foot projecting from the vehicle's open driver's-side door.

The garage bay to the left is empty. An oil stain has bicycle tracks and footprints running through it. The footwear impressions are singular and nondescript with no tread pattern. Sam picks up a bottle of motor oil and small toolbox to place parallel to the tracks, preserving them from traffic until we can get photographs. To the right, behind the closed garage door sits a yellow car, engine off, but the radio DJ is jabbering away. The perimeter of the garage is cluttered with a lawnmower and small yard tools as well as large toys, two bicycles, a tool bench, and stacked cardboard boxes.

The car, one of the officers tells us as he stands outside the garage, is a 1970 Mach 1, 428 Cobra-Jet Mustang, and the color is "Grabber" yellow, a limited edition. He goes on. "It's a Shaker Scoop top-loader four-speed."

I hear Mick Jagger. The classic rock station appropriate for this vehicle belts out *Sympathy for the Devil*, right on cue. I wonder if anyone else notices.

The car-buff cop tells us the high-performance engine 'runs rich' and caused the engine to overheat long before it could run out of gas.

"The only way to get gas to the engine faster would be with a garden hose," he informs us.

The repetitious *doot doos* of the sorrowful music fills the otherwise quiet of the garage, giving the pathetic woman a haunting farewell song.

"She only gets about five miles to the gallon. God! I would have killed for a car like this in high school!" Everyone turns to look at him and he shuts up, but he can't resist adding one more thing. "Her husband told me this car was her pride and joy."

The bare foot with pink polished toenails and a clean sole protrudes from the open car door. Following the length of her bare legs, I see the cheeks of her butt peering beneath the short Daisy Duke cutoffs. The midsection of her body is draped across the console, her shoulders and head rest in the passenger seat with the back of her right hand propped against the armrest of the closed passenger door. A mass of long blonde hair covers her face. I make a notation of her position. Sam looks in the windows and encounters no difficulty moving from the rear to the passenger side. The precious vehicle is afforded all the space necessary to keep it protected from accidental dings or scratches. His eyes meet mine through the windows. This is not suicide. The unnatural position of the body suggests she was placed in the car after she was already unconscious. Her bright pink skin is evidence of carbon monoxide poisoning—she was definitely still breathing when placed in the car. The non-verbal communication between us continues. We get on with processing the scene.

I've been Sam's spear gatherer for so long I can anticipate his every move. After a cursory search in the interior of the house, we return to the garage. Back at the van, I stuff a few small rulers in a pocket, grab a tripod, and the old dinosaur of a camera. Use of these cameras requires photographic know-how most crime scene people no longer possess. Knowing I have full control, no automation to screw things up, I set the proper aperture for the lighting, screw the tripod onto the base of the camera, and hold it like a freezer pop. I start with overall shots. *General to specific*, Sam has drilled those words into my head so much they will probably be on my tombstone. I photograph the exterior, including the house number, and make my way back through the house. Startled by the crunch of a wayward glass bead underfoot in the laundry room, I move rapidly into the garage.

Sam saunters up beside me and quietly declares, "You'll need scale photographs of those footwear impressions." He points to the oily patterned stains. "That seems to be the only evidence of an intruder." I produce a ruler and wiggle it in front of him. "And Megan, check the shoes of all the officers who've been in the garage and make a note of the eliminations."

Photographs of her feet are in order. No oil or dirt proves it's highly unlikely she walked across the garage floor. Sam begins by processing the entrances to the house for fingerprints. Even though he's sure it's not a suicide, he doesn't make it known to others present. He won't say until he's asked. The one to ask will be Hap. I make my way into the house, and through the front window, I catch a glimpse of the media across the street, setting up their cameras, pointing them in our direction. My mother says she's tired of seeing my backside on the Channel 5 News. Her religious loyalty to the network station is hinged on the recent addition of a good-looking weatherman.

The body snatchers from the Tarrant County Mortician Service are also waiting impatiently in the alleyway to do their job and get to the next deceased-person call. I open the passenger's side door, not knowing whether her hand will fall or remain upright. The path of rigor is predictable. It travels from the head and neck to the extremities, and then leaves the extremities, returning to the trunk before entering the neck and diminishing. But at this point, I'm unsure, given the temperature and time since death, just where the rigor lies. Luckily, her hand falls slowly. It almost touches my leg and I jump back to avoid it. I don't touch dead people, and they definitely don't touch me. Hap chuckles. I hadn't noticed he was watching me. I wish I could go to him and he would hold me, making this growing nightmare go away. The fantasy of being enveloped in his arms gives me the strength to finish my task.

Sam walks close to me and asks if I need anything else before he lets the attendants take the body. I shake my head and he waves them in. I readjust the F-stop on the camera to get pictures of the removal of the body from the car. Gloved hands grab her ankles and pull. Ready arms catch the weight of her hips and place her on the waiting gurney. *Flash. Wind. Flash. Wind. Repeat as fast as possible.*

As the formality unfolds, so does her body—with effort. The attendants straighten her knees and hips with a sickening crack and snap so she'll lie flat on the gurney. One of them slides his hand under the veil of hair to reveal a face I must photograph. I move in close, and whatever is keeping me vertical decides it's time to go horizontal. "Megan!" Hap calls my name, and everything goes black.

8

"Megan, are you alright?" I recognize the voice, but it doesn't match the face staring into mine with a penlight and stethoscope around his neck. "Oh God, let me up." I struggle to sit, pushing the paramedic aside.

"Sweetheart, wait just a second, they need to make sure you're okay." Hap's emotional plea masks the concern he should feel for a coworker.

I throw my left foot to the floor of the ambulance and brace myself so the spinning in my head will stop. I put my hands under my butt and heave myself up. Hap catches me again, my head buried in his chest, and lays me back on the gurney.

"Megan lie down. You passed out and you've been out awhile. Let the paramedics do their job." He motions for the attendant and exits the ambulance. I don't quite understand what has happened, but I know I don't want to be here.

～

In solitude at home, I put Annie Lennox in the CD player and she reminds me I am no longer capable of love. I turn up the volume and drown out the world.

Connor is home early from his dad's and asleep. True to character, his dad drank too much, and Connor asked his stepmom to bring him home because he couldn't handle it. He tells me as much after a good night's rest and my obligatory rub of his head. "Mornin' Punkin'!"

"Urgh!" Shooing me off, he sips from his coffee. It looks more like tinged milk than my caffeine jolts. He hates morning.

~

Sunday, October 30, 1994

Lazy Sunday, Hap calls me at home. "Hey, let's have lunch tomorrow at the little café over on Henderson... Summer's, okay? You know where I'm talking about? Up from the Academy?"

"Yeah, sure I know where it is." I'm stunned to hear from him. He knows something. "Why are you calling me at home?" The words spill out as I realize I'm just being paranoid. I don't allow him to answer. "Never mind. Sure, I'll have lunch, but why don't we go somewhere with decent food?"

In defense of his favorite cop eatery, he responds. "What do ya mean? They've got the best lunch specials in town. Everybody eats there."

By 'everybody,' he means all of his buddies. The old cops always took their trainees there, and it became habit, hanging out in the safe company of fellow officers.

"I'll bring Jackie. What did you think of her? I can't believe, in all my years on the force, the only trainees I got were young, trigger-happy, wet-behind-the-ear boys, and now that I'm too old to dare think about fooling around, they give me someone like her." His rough, deep laugh rumbles and a small twinge of jealousy prickles my heart. "I feel as though I'm spending all my time fighting off every other man just to protect her integrity."

I butt in. "You? Too old? Never!"

His voice is as sensual in a Texan way as Sean Connery's is in a Scottish way. I hope he does bring Jackie. Her presence will fade the heat from me. I know he wants to talk about Kacy's murder and my ex-husband. I don't know how much Sam told him, and I don't want to discuss my past, with him or anyone.

~

Monday, October 31, 1994, 11:15 a.m.

I push on the glass door while reading PULL. The large, orange pumpkin wearing a pointy black hat taped to the glass hides my embarrassment. As I enter, I look around to see if anyone was watching my mistake. I try to recover, like when a cat falls not so gracefully and acts like the blunder was meant for amusement. With a smile, I catch Hap's eyes. He *was* watching. Thankfully, the diner is empty except for him. It's still early, the lunch crowd yet to descend. He slurps steaming coffee as I slide into the vinyl booth and feel the coolness on my thighs. During his repeated attempts to quit smoking, coffee becomes his crutch, and he drinks it all day, every day, no matter how rancid.

The waitress is on my heels. "What'll you have to drink?"

"Iced tea, please." My friendly tone disturbs her.

She reminds me of Flo, the wiry, brazen waitress on the old sitcom, *Alice*, from years ago. Her platinum hair solidified with hairspray looks brittle to the touch. I glance at her nametag, Judy. The mini jukebox on the wall provides a distraction to avoid eye contact with Hap.

"Listen girl, you've got to tell me what's going on." Palms down, he leans in. "Something's up, and I want to know what it is!" He snags my chin between thumb and forefinger, turning my face to his.

I pull away and turn to thank the waitress as she places a jumbo-size glass of tea in front of me. She pinches a straw from her apron and presents it to me with a smirk of unworthiness.

"You amaze me." I flip the plastic menu open and closed, clicking the metal edges together with each flap. "Look at you, multi-talented, busy cop on the go, and you still have time to be so concerned about little ol' me." A compliment was a good distraction. "Where's Jackie? I thought you were bringing her today."

"She'll be here. Now stop avoiding the question. What's going on?"

With a confused look on my face, I say I'm doing great. "Going on with what?"

"You know what I'm talking about!" A shy smile creeps across his face, I think he's blushing. His eyes catch mine and there is no escape, the swimming pool-blue clarity has a paralyzing effect on me.

The waitress returns to break the spell. She speaks to Hap as if I'm not sitting in front of her, "So Sweetie, what'll it be today?"

I suppose Hap never comes here with a woman. Judging from the jealousy in her mannerism toward me, his wedding ring is no deterrent. Maybe they have a thing. He rarely talks about his wife, Sylvia. I've heard through the grapevine she's agoraphobic and lost her delicate grip with reality after losing a child early in the marriage. His role in their relationship became that of a caretaker more than husband. If I know anything about Hap, I know he's almost as devoted to me as he is to his wife. He provides me with intellectual stimulus without expectation of a sexual relationship. He'd rescue me from the depths of hell if I asked, and I would do the same for him in a heartbeat.

Hap orders the Tuesday lunch, even though it's Monday. They serve set lunches on certain days of the week, every week. If you can't remember what it is, I guess you get a lunch surprise. Flo shoots me a look of preeminence without a word. I order vegetable soup. She jots down the order, spins on a heel, and disappears.

"Are you feeling better, today? I've been worried." Sure, he probably watched football all weekend and didn't give me a second thought after lifting the phone to request my presence here today.

"I'm great. Couldn't be better... How 'bout those Cowboys? What do you think, they gonna make it to the Super Bowl this year?" I chuckle to myself. I've managed to put him off, and I see Jackie *pulling* the door open as several masculine hands reach over her head to help with the door. I know they'll all expect to sit close. Our private conversation is now over.

"Hey, Boss!" one of them shouts to Hap as he walks up to the booth.

I raise my gaze to meet Hap's, put my finger to my lips, and whisper. "Oh well, maybe later."

The old wooden chair legs make loud scraping noises on the asphalt tile floor as everyone takes their place at a table nearby. Jackie escapes the whole ordeal, excusing herself to the restroom. When she returns, a couple of the detectives stand to offer her the chair between them. She looks at Hap for rescue, but he doesn't offer any. The crowd begins throwing their orders at a skinny waitress. She doesn't miss a beat, and with abbreviated dictation she heads for the kitchen.

An investigator with the auto task force asks Jackie about the homicide a couple of weeks ago. She's good... she pretends she doesn't know what he's talking about. I wonder if it's just for Hap's benefit, or if she really isn't going to tell them anything about it.

"Well... I hear tell it was set up to look like a suicide, by the ex-husband. He put her in her classic Mustang and left the engine running in the garage. I heard it's the same guy that killed the woman down off Hulen Street. I think he strung her up or something, didn't he?" The forceful cop was talking so loud and fast no one could shut him up.

"Yeah, that was his first wife, and the one this weekend was his second wife," another one chimed in.

"Hey, you guys!" Jackie can't hold it in. "Where did you get your information or the idea it was murder? From Channel 5 or the Startlegram?" It's a common nickname for *The Star-Telegram*, an often-mocked newspaper. "She had carbon monoxide poisoning, that's all we know. The Medical Examiner hasn't issued an autopsy report yet... and by the way, your gossip and innuendos are irritating, to say the least." She lifts her purse from the back of the chair and joins Hap and me.

The quiet is broken as she scoots into the booth next to me. The abrasive cop assumes she was one of them, and when she doesn't just go along with their guesstimating, he lashes out. "Yeah and Kacy Flannery hung herself. It's too much of a cowinkydink, if you ask me." The smartass cop just isn't about to let Jackie have the last word.

"All I can say," another one interjects, "I wish I could set my ex-wife up with this guy."

The whole table burst with laughter. Jackie looks at me with sorrowful eyes. There's no way she can understand what I'm feeling. The memories of embarrassment and looks of pity reemerge, but at least they don't know I'm one of those exes. She doesn't know. Or does she? I look at Hap, wondering what he knows, what Sam has told him. What has *he* told Jackie? Silence hangs uncomfortably over our table throughout the meal. I pay the waitress and when she brings the change, I plop a couple of quarters in the jukebox, push some buttons, and excuse myself. I squeeze between the jacket-draped chairs of criminal intellect's table and ours. *Sentimental Journey* begins to play. I swing my hips in time to the music as I head for the door. I look back and catch every one of the men turned to see the view.

I return to the lab, grateful to have escaped the paws of a playful kitten when I'm ordered into the cage with the claws of a tiger. Our secretary, MaryJo, raises her eyes above her glasses with bowed head and says, "Sam wants to see you, and by the way, he's not in a good mood."

"When the hell were you gonna tell me who *this* woman is— or was?" The wall behind him is a patchwork of framed news articles, commendations and award plaques. Most prominently displayed and the largest item is Sam's undergraduate degree from Texas Tech University in 1970. The first class to graduate after the name changed from College to University, at his request, he jokes. A West Texas incarnate whose blood runs Raider Red, and today it's boiling. I'm caught totally off guard by his request to see me when I return from lunch. I haven't had time to consider what he wants from me or what I should say.

Before I sit, he tosses the autopsy photos of the cherry-colored woman on his cluttered desk in front of me. They slide and a few cascade to the floor. Instinctively, I stoop and retrieve the images of Missy's innards exposed.

He's linked events. "That's why you fainted isn't it? Hell, Megan, the guys are all placing bets that you're pregnant. Throwing up on the bushes and then fainting." A metallic clink rings out each time he pokes the lamp illuminating the mess on his desk. "They're all wondering who's gonna be a daddy." His arm sweeps past the trophy wall to indicate the entire general public. "I knew about Kacy, but not about this one. Why didn't you tell me?"

Sam talks so quickly my thoughts can't catch up. What does he know? I wish he'd just say it.

"Maybe it's best everyone thinks you are pregnant for now— until we sort this out." He flops into his chair with an exasperated sigh and digs through the clutter on his desk.

I shoot back, "Is that what Hap and Jackie think? Is that the reason for lunch today? Their uneasiness and pitiful looks? They think I'm a poor thirty-six-year-old single mother of teenagers unfortunately and unexpectedly pregnant?"

"We've got to piece this together. Megan, I have to know what you know. Who is Missy to you, to your ex…"

"Wait, just a minute… are you implying that I sleep around?" Before I can defend myself from his flippant degradation, he gives up the search and snatches the telephone handset from its base.

"Well, you are divorced!" He holds his hands in midair with

a matter-of-fact expression. Like I should agree with his forgone conclusion? I don't think Sam means the comment as a personal jab, only implying that's the way the world sees me. Its normal speak for him, just as all Mexicans are spics, homosexuals are fags, a divorcee is a trollop. "Hap needs to be here. You're gonna tell us everything!" His index finger stabs the buttons.

9

"*H*e's at Summer's, I just left him there."

Sam slams the receiver down and yells, "MaryJo! Get a hold of Hap—he's at Summer's."

I shuffle through the autopsy photos of Missy. What nice round breasts she has. She and I have some things in common, but anatomy isn't one of them. She is—*was*—very petite, never an extra pound. I, on the other hand, have a tall athletic build and practically flat chest with sturdy childbearing hips. The graceful body of a dancer, my mother says. The two things we did have in common were our hair, long and thick, and we both were once married to Kurt, as was Kacy.

Sam spots his pipe and chocolate-brown kid leather tobacco pouch, the one I gave him for Christmas last year. With irate gestures, he stuffs the bowl. "You free this afternoon? Don't have anything pressing, do you?"

Sam ignores the city council's ban on smoking in public buildings, and he will until Fort Worth City Code Compliance physically removes every semblance of tobacco from his office. Not likely, since several city and county officials still smoke in their offices. Sadly, for their health, Fort Worth is inept at enforcing changes in socially acceptable behaviors.

I make a feeble attempt to straighten Missy's file and place it in the only bare spot on his desk. I remind myself each time I'm in his office—there is a method to his messiness.

"No. Well, I'm on call for court, but you know how that goes," I finally reply.

Most drug cases plead out. When a defendant realizes the cost of going to trial and how unsympathetic juries are to drug offenders, they usually take the offered plea. Prosecutors place me on call a couple of days a week, but I rarely testify. I'm hoping today will be one of those days.

"Okay, then be here, in my office," he taps the Timex on his wrist, "at three. We're gonna get this out in the open and deal with it." He dismisses me and pulls an old shoe from one of the unsealed paper sacks littering the floor beside him.

Reluctantly, I return to my office and add a shaky signature to each of the newly typed reports left on my desk. While formulating a statement, I straighten my office and organize my pile of unfinished cases according to who's hollering the loudest for results. Cleaning calms my nerves and structures my thoughts. The steady flow of drug cases ensures job security, but at the moment, I'm feeling unsure of Sam's plan for me. I prioritize the possessions I'll pack first.

On the way back to Sam's office, my left foot yearns to cut and run while my right strides with confidence. The repetitive mental rehearsal of my carefully chosen words helps me fight the desire to sprint for the door. I envision a lone chair under a dangling, bright, bare bulb as I pass MaryJo's desk and brace myself for the inquisition. The door moans in protest as I push it open. Hap and Sam don't notice. My heightened sense of awareness tempts me to retrieve the WD40 from behind Sam. The can sits abandoned among a recent assembly of used shoes, butcher paper, a fingerprint brush, and a jar of black powder. But I don't. I wonder when he'll finish creating the comparison footwear patterns. Chances are the project will become another task left undone in this room.

A well-chewed toothpick protrudes from Hap's toothy grin as he casually slumps in the corner chair, left ankle propped on right knee. Seated behind his desk, Sam administers fretful taps to the tobacco in his pipe. Their attention turns to me, and discussion on the mobile home murder ceases.

"We'll get back to this later." Hap leans up to the desk and pounds the thick handful of photographs into a neat brick before stuffing them in the flimsy paper envelope with their negatives. Sam mindlessly fingers his lighter, hesitant to ignite the prepared bowl. It's obvious his addiction to nicotine is battling his conscious effort to help his friend quit this nasty habit.

Beside Hap, the green patent-leather chair I occupied earlier waits for me, sans the overhead bulb. Missy's case folder rests untouched in the same spot. An uncomfortable silence amplifies normally unnoticed sirens and traffic sounds. I racked my brain for two hours figuring out what to say. I structured and practiced my intended words repeatedly. What could I leave out? Just how much do I want them to know? All of it was a nightmare, a part of my life I'd rather forget.

"Are we gonna play question and answer?" I ask to break the tension.

"No, no, you just start at the beginning and tell us everything," Hap says sternly.

"Whether you think it's relevant or not, just tell us." Sam seems flustered and angry with me. "At this point you obviously don't feel much is relevant or you would've already told us."

"Please don't be angry," I plead. "I never wanted to tell anyone about this shit!" My head falls to my hands and I watch his penny loafers withdraw. "I don't want to remember it or relive it. I want it to go away!"

Hap's expectant expression prods. I take a deep breath and start my reasoning. "Years of living in a dysfunctional, alcoholic home made me a peacemaker, always walking on eggshells, never wanting anyone to be upset. Omitting truths kept the peace. I guess I thought when something undesirable happened, if we never talked about it, then it's like it never happened. I just wanted a normal life, like everyone else." I turn to Sam and inquire, "What does he know?" pointing at Hap with my thumb like a hitchhiker.

"We haven't talked much. He knows about Kacy," Sam says. "And we've learned about Missy from everyone but you!"

"Hell, darling, I bet twenty bucks you were pregnant." Hap's laugh bellows in the confines of Sam's office. "But I don't think Sam would hold a Pow-wow for that, unless, well, who's the father?" He looks at Sam and then back at me.

In one sentence, his words bring me down from what I had become to a woman sleeping with a noteworthy man too stupid to use birth control. I start to get angry. I figure in a few minutes he'll be the one feeling about three inches tall. Why lower myself? My admiration of him drops a few points. I'll soon forgive him though. This is the kind of disability suffered by white men his age raised in the South by sexist fathers who believe women are chattel. I respect the fact he's evolved quite far from that attitude. Not completely, but a remarkable distance.

"Missy Diane Holt, Kacy Renee Flannery, April Elaine Cox, and Sarah Megan Brooks were all married to Kurt Terrell at some point in their miserable little lives. Now two of us are dead and two of us are still alive. Well, one at least that I'm certain of." I begin with no intention of stopping until the whole story passes my lips. "Kacy was the first wife, Missy the second, April the third and then me, the fourth."

I take a breath and continue. "I haven't heard from any of them in a long time. Except April, and that's been a couple of years. She's a nut case. Still sent letters to my house for months after Kurt disappeared."

"Wait! Hold on!" Hap interrupts me. "You're telling me that the two dead women knew each other, and you, and you all—all four of you—used to be married to the same guy, and then one day he just disappeared?"

"Yeah, just disappeared." My palms land on my thighs. I straighten my spine, a futile effort to remove stress. "One day he up and walked away."

"Why? How? Why didn't you tell me any of this, Megan?" Hap cuts me off again. "I can't believe in all the years I've known you, never a word about this. Not one fucking word!" He slaps the arms of his chair and mumbles. "I'll be goddamned!"

"Well that's a long story. Do you want the short version?" I notice a pebble stuck in the tread of Hap's shoe. I fight the urge to pick it free. "I told him to clean up the shit pile he turned our lives into, but he chose to leave it instead, about six years ago, plain and simple."

"Hold up Megan." Sam leans back, eyes his unlit pipe and stretches his legs. The worn loafers reappear. "Back to the others, we'll get to that later."

"Wait, wait, back up Megan! You married a man who'd been married three times before?" Hap says disbelieving, or condescending, I can't tell. I'm glad he finds it hard to believe. At least he thinks I'm too smart to do something so idiotic, even if I'm not.

"Actually, I didn't know, Hap," I say in a condescending manner. "It was during a weird time in my life. You've been stupid in love, haven't you?" I remember to whom I'm talking.

"Never mind," Hap's brow wrinkles at the thought. "No, no, can't say I have. I barely remember what it's like to be in love. I think I'd remember *stupid* in love. That's a new one." He shakes his head.

I know he'll never understand, so I quit trying. "And he has four children. Fortunately, we didn't have any children together. What else can I say? He loves women. He knows how to seduce women. He's a romantic—nice dinners, flowers, very generous." *This* is even more difficult to explain. How could I not fall for such a man?

"So let me see if I've got this straight? This Kurt is an addict.

He's addicted to women, he uses 'em up and throws 'em away.
Is that 'bout right?" Hap looks at me.

Sam agrees. "Sounds that way to me."

10

The emotion of a Valentine's memory summons tears. I pull a rough paper towel from my lab coat pocket and dab, gently preserving what's left of today's makeup. One bitterly cold Valentine's Day, I arrived to an empty house, no kids or husband. There was a note tied to a lone red balloon floating in the middle of the living room that read, "Your bath awaits, My Lady." I undressed as I walked to the bedroom, dropping articles of clothing like Hansel and Gretel dropped bread-crumbs. Totally nude by the time I reached the bathroom, I found the garden tub filled with towering bubbles, steam rising. A sweating glass of wine and a hair clip sat on the edge of the tub illuminated by candles. He thought of everything. I slid into the sweet-smelling water, absorbing the experience. Warm to the core, I relaxed as soft music played. Kurt squeezed behind and placed his legs on either side of me. His massage started at my shoulders and traveled downward.

We dried off a little and fell on the bed in a tangle of arms and legs. I landed on my back and saw dozens of red balloons floating at different heights all around the bedroom. A little pastel heart-shaped note was tied to each one. "Be Mine," "Kiss Me," and "I Love You" dangled and bobbed all around us as we made love. Wafts of garlic from the kitchen filled my nostrils. A dinner of decadence followed—lasagna, wine, and being fed tiramisu one slow, sumptuous, teasing bite at a time.

HAP CLEARS HIS THROAT, snapping me back to the present. "The Kurt I fell in love with paid attention to the details of pleasure." I close my eyes and roll my head from side to side, feeling the tension in my neck ease. My gaze centers on the mascara-stained paper towel twisted in my fingers. I look up and see they're both waiting for me to recover from the sobs. Lost in thought, I sweep my hair back into a knot, let it go, and brush away the remnants of tears. Every woman I told about that Valentine's Day understood, but I know Sam and Hap just won't get it.

"The first couple of years we were together were the happiest days of my life. He was so attentive to my every need. Then one day, it all started to unravel. He didn't come home some nights, he'd ask me for money, and then he'd spend money we didn't have. You wouldn't believe the enormous amounts he charged on my credit cards. Within six months, our relationship deterio-rated to arguments about money and responsibility. After he left, I found out he'd lost his job and had been embezzling money from his investors." I watch for their responses before I go on. "He had worked for an oil-and-gas securities brokerage firm in Dallas. He was getting threatening phone calls at home. I didn't understand why, and he wouldn't talk to me about it. I couldn't handle it."

I try to get as much out as I can without getting into too much detail. "The stress was horrible at that point. I had no idea how much worse it was going to get before it could get better." My gaze drifts up to the ceiling, the dingy acoustic texture is easier to focus on than their judgmental stares. Hap lays his hand on mine and pats it.

"Jesus, Megan!" His look of pity opens the flood gate and my sobs become spastic.

"Once he left and was no longer intercepting mail or putting off bill collectors, the enormity of debt became all too evident." I fail to mention the amount.

Sam leans on his forearms holding the pipe in both hands. "How much money are we talking about?"

"In total, about $75,000 to the IRS, with penalties and interest around $50,000. They put a lien on my home. I was fortunate to be a student working part-time jobs. I cleaned houses and was paid cash they never knew about, but they threatened to garnish my wages from my job at school for taxes he never paid. I argued the bulk of the unpaid taxes were before we were even married." Trembling, I wipe tears with the damp surrogate tissue. "But you know what? The IRS doesn't really care about details. They just want their money."

Anger swells, but I persist in pushing aside the most traumatic part of my story, an experience that severed soul from body. The part that left an empty pain that money couldn't fix and time failed to heal. The part that culminated with an immeasurable hatred for Kurt Terrell. The part that, if left unspoken, never happened.

"And it got worse. When bill collectors called, all I could do was cry. I told them my husband abandoned me with incredible debt including the IRS, and I told them 'the IRS will get whatever I have long before you do'." I shift my weight back to the center of the saggy chair. The springs creak, and the leather feels cool.

"And usually before I hung up the phone, the person on the other end was comforting me. They'd tell me to keep my chin up, everything will be alright. Sometimes, they would promise to place a note on my case, and they wouldn't call anymore. Other times they'd just call and hang up.

"And Connor, poor Connor. Kurt had been the head coach of his Little League team. He left the team with no goodbyes, no explanation. Connor was so brave. His teammates taunted him. I tried to get him to leave the team, but he wouldn't. He toughed it out for the rest of the season. Do you know how hard that was for a nine-year-old boy? He was so disappointed." I gasp for air and blow my stuffed nose.

"And then, our dog died. We all were heartbroken." With that, I laugh through the tears. "You hear that in all sob stories. It sounds cliché, but it really happened."

"It sounds like a country western song." Hap adds with a chuckle. "Hell, girl you should sell this story to Randy Travis."

"I kept hoping the worst of it was over. What else could possibly happen?" My hell had just begun, but I can't tell them about it. I can't tell anyone about it. "My life was…" My laughs relapse to tears.

Hap finishes my sentence. "In shambles, your life was a total fucking wreck!" He lays a hand on my head and brushes my hair back with the coarseness of his rough palm.

"Yeah it was. Thanks for pointing that out." My fingertips caress the bumpy metal tacks on the arms of the chair, fighting the temptation to reach for Hap.

Sam breaks the silence. "Geez, Megan, I never knew you'd been through so much." Reminded of Sam's presence, Hap reels in his compassion.

"I loved him, but our lives weren't going in the same direction. Mine was headed toward crime-fighting and his to prison time." I sit tall on the edge of the chair and tuck my feet under it. I pushed my fists, filled with soggy paper crumbles, into the depths of my lab coat pockets.

"Since he left I've tried very hard to put this behind me. I filed bankruptcy and successfully paid all of his back taxes and debt." I feel drained and think I've said enough.

That's when the interrogation begins. Hap starts. "Where did you meet this guy?"

I repeat everything I'd told Sam previously and add some, leave out some. When I fail to include something, Sam quickly pipes in with, "What about..." I backtrack and fill in the gaps until Sam is satisfied. I had explained Kacy and Missy to Sam earlier, but left out my discovery of the third wife, April. So, I tell them what I pieced together about Kurt and April.

"Kurt met April at Billy Bob's. She asked him for a ride home one night, and he obliged, being the gentleman that he is. When they got in his truck, he found out she meant his home not hers, and she wouldn't go away. She became pregnant and he married her. The marriage didn't last as long as the pregnancy. They were separated when I started to date him and he didn't bother to tell me about her or the baby. I guess the divorce was final before our wedding." I'm tired but I go on. The sooner I finish, the sooner I can put this day behind me.

"A few days after Kurt gave me a huge diamond ring that I later found out he bought on my credit card, a woman approached me as I came out of the post office. She showed me pictures of a newborn. I thought she was just some crazy woman. I looked at her pictures smiling, telling her what a cute baby. She asked me if I thought he looked like his father. I said I wasn't sure since I didn't know his father. She became very disturbed and told me the father was Kurt. When I confronted Kurt about it, he said she was a crazy old girlfriend and it wasn't his baby. He said that's why he never told me about her or the baby.

"He kept her away from me after that and I didn't hear from her again until after he left. She showed up at my front door, about six weeks after he'd gone, demanding to see him. I thought she was just plain nuts. I asked her to come in and tried to calm her down. That's when she told me all about their short marriage, and how he promised to support her and the baby if she would just stay away. Apparently, they were going hungry. She was unable to work because of her mental health. I suggested she contact Aid for Dependent Children and gave her the phone number of the state welfare department. With that, she left and I haven't seen her since, just an occasional letter accusing me of knowing Kurt's whereabouts."

I finish as it's getting dark out. Daylight Saving recently started and, although I know it's not really late, it seems like it is. Hap continues his questions about Kurt's upbringing. "What kind of parents did he have?"

Exhaustion and hunger add to my emotional state as I recall Kurt's unhappy past. "Well, he was adopted when he was four. He told me he was taken from his parents after the New Mexico Child Protective Services found he had been singled out by his mother and suffered horrible abuses. He remembers most of it vividly. What he was too young to remember his sister told him about. Their mother burned him with cigarettes while he sat strapped in his high chair."

They look at me intently and then at each other. "He told me how it felt to drown and see a face through the fingers that held his head under water. He'd struggle for his young life and then miraculously be plucked from death by unknown hands. What started as innocent caretaking events turned into torturous attempts to end his life. He was hardly old enough to recognize the face that hated him so much." I relay the incidences he shared, devoid of the compassion and sympathy I felt initially. I just feel cold.

"He discovered he was adopted shortly before his adoptive mother's death when he was sixteen. Rummaging through some old papers, he found the names of his biological parents on an original birth certificate. He felt twice betrayed, once by the woman that tortured him and again by the woman who raised him. Even though she was very ill, cancer, I think." I shift my weight from one cheek to the other again and go on. "All those years he thought she was the woman responsible for the horrible memories. He grew up hating his adoptive mother, he would not let himself love her or get close enough to be hurt again."

"We need to get a psychologist; you know one of those profiler guys from the FBI." Hap looks at Sam for confirmation.

I've known Sam long enough to know his opinion of forensic psychologists. He doesn't have much faith in their generic diagnoses. Their abstract theories are very subjective. *White male, between the ages of 28 and 35, loner, injured animals as a child,* blah, blah, blah. Can't say I've seen anything amazing in their profiling either. I'd read a few books on the subject and, although it makes for interesting reading, I'd never heard they actually caught someone based on profiling.

I know Hap will have his way on this, being the lead investigator on these cases. I also know Sam won't share his doubts on the subject. For Sam, only tangible evidence subject to analysis has true bearing in a criminal case. We argue this point again and again. He reminds me, my responsibility as a scientist is to collect, preserve, and interpret physical evidence, nothing more.

One case taught me to pick my battles with Sam carefully. An ex-police officer claimed his wife, a successful attorney, shot herself in the chest hours after informing him she'd filed for divorce. His attempts at CPR destroyed useful blood spatter evidence. He covered the evidence of his crime with more blood. With a history of physical abuse, I thought it was a well-staged homicide. Sam's contention was the physical evidence did not support a homicide. The jury agreed with me, he got 30 years. I learned not to gloat. He didn't speak to me for a week.

Sam's a good witness for either side. He remains focused on the evidence. I agree he's right to a certain extent. The physical evidence will tell the tale of events, but when that evidence is lacking, or altered in some way, one must rely on other areas and judge what happened. People do change crime scenes, sometimes intentionally and other times not.

"Go on," Hap says. "Did he ever find his real mother?"

"Yes." I rub my eyes and yawn. "But shouldn't I be telling this to a psychologist instead of y'all?"

"Yeah, I think you've told us enough for now. I'm puzzled though. Why now? Why do you think Kurt's resurfaced after all these years?" Sam's rhetorical question hangs. "I'll look into the fraud charges… maybe the statute of limitations is up or maybe he finally cracked!" Hap makes a hacking sound in the back of his throat and jerks his head to one side in an attempt to imitate a crazy person.

"Maybe these two aren't his first victims?" Sam rolls his eyes at Hap's suggestion. An uneasy feeling sweeps over me. My stomach growls and I tame it with a pat. "Okay, I'll agree we can stop for now," Hap concedes. "But Megan, until we get some assurance that these deaths aren't related, I think you should be very careful." The cop in Hap shines through. My big protector stands as he gives commands. "You're not to be alone at any time. If you need an escort somewhere, call me, if I can't be there, I'll find someone, an officer to watch you."

"What?" I don't believe what I'm hearing. "To… watch me?"

"Yes, if you're at home alone, lock all the doors and windows, pull the drapes and…" As he rambles on, I cut him off.

"No! I am quite capable of looking after myself. I always lock my doors, but I refuse to let fear rule my life. If you're so concerned with my safety, find him—find Kurt! Ask him why all this is happening. Ask him why he screws up everything, every woman that ever loved him." My anger is so strong I can no longer hold back the emotion.

With increasing volume, I demand, "Ask him why he left me, why he fucked up my life, and abandoned me." I smear angry tears with the back of my hand. "If he killed Kacy and Missy, he's got to be close. Doesn't take a genius to figure that out! I bet he's within an hour of Fort Worth."

I stomp past Hap toward the door and point up in his face. "Show us what a good detective you are, Hap! Find the unfind-able! That will keep me safe!" I turn to Sam. "Can I go now?" He nods, a bit bewildered at my outburst. "Let me know when the psychologist is ready for me." I head to my office to retrieve my purse and keys, drained.

Hap adores me, and I feel horrible for speaking to him so harshly. A serologist calls to me on her way out. I hold back tears, wave, and fake a genuine farewell. "Have a good evening." No sooner do I shut my office door than Hap opens it.

"Megan…" Even with my back to him, his deep voice is as comforting as his presence is ominous. The concern in his voice touches me. I struggle to remove my lab coat, turning the sleeves inside out as his hands hang in midair, not knowing how or *if* he should help me. I throw it to a chair and brush past him.

He grips my shoulder. "Tell me, what can I do to help you?"

Wincing in pain, I want to ask, *Can you unbreak my heart and make me whole again?*

"Not now!" It's all I can say. No one can understand the love paired with immense hate I harbor for Kurt. I don't understand it, and I can't explain it, not now. Not ever.

11

TUESDAY, NOVEMBER 8, 1994

*T*he appointment for my interview with a forensic psychologist was set up within a week. With two murders attributed to one killer, it wasn't hard convincing the FBI to send Dr. Edie Mann. She's a short, full woman with a cherubic face and straight black hair past her waist. Her intermittent unruly grey hairs are determined to make their presence known among the mass. She's wearing a flowing dress of loden green gauze that hangs to her ankles and strappy flat sandals, definitely a flower child.

Her handshake is firm. "Please, call me Edie." She brings me close enough to detect a hint of vanilla and patchouli perfume and motions for me to sit. We arranged to meet in her room at the old Texas Hotel downtown. This hotel used to hide the fact that President John F. Kennedy slept his last night here, ashamed of Fort Worth's part in that sad time. Now the shame we shared with our neighbor to the east has subsided, and it appears this hotel's stake in history is sellable. The corridors prominently display enlarged photos of John and Jackie's stay in Fort Worth. This hotel is a far cry from the Holiday Inn where I'll stay next week for the conference in Oklahoma City.

Dr. Mann's suite is outfitted with mahogany paneling and

built-in matching bookcases. The faux cowhide chairs look comfortable, but itchy. The sofa is tan, suede-like upholstery, and I take a seat there. She turns one of the chairs to face the sofa and sits. Edie is easy to talk to, and I like her right away. I suspect Hap requested a woman psychologist after witnessing my frustration trying to make him and Sam understand stupid in love. We quickly establish a good rapport, through "get to know you" chit-chat, sharing our children's names, ages, and whereabouts.

Edie wants to delve into Kurt's past right off the bat. I briefly explain what I'd told Sam and Hap. She questions me about our marriage, sex life, and his day-to-day habits. She asks some things I think are rather ridiculous, but I answer them anyway. "When I knew him, he was neat, but not to the point of being anal. He paid close attention to his appearance, especially his hair." I point to my hairline. "He has a premature grey streak at the forehead above his right eye. His clothes weren't expensive, but he always looked very distinguished, even in jeans. He likes to wear boots and jeans and starched shirts—not Western shirts, just regular shirts with button-down collars. He's a head-turner. Men as well as women notice him. He appears successful, polished and sincere."

"The grey would help give him that." She pauses to mull over what I've told her for a long minute. "Why did he leave? Hap said something about some unhappy investors... in oil and gas ventures?"

"Yes. He was the only registered broker working with an oil-and-gas exploration company called HiTech, and then they changed the name to Explorer Something—I can't remember the rest of the name." I cross my legs, wishing I'd chosen a firmer place to sit.

She taps her pen on the notepad resting on her knee. "Was it a lot of money? Did these investors lose a lot?"

It takes me a second to answer the compilation of questions. "Well, after he was gone, an investigator from the Mississippi Attorney General's Office contacted me. He wanted to know if I had any of Kurt's files. I told him they were stacked in my garage. He asked if I'd send them to him. I asked him how much money. You know, like how big are we talking here?"

My throat is dry, and I look around for some water but don't see any, so I continue. "When he told me hundreds of thousands of dollars, I guess he sensed my surprise and told me not to worry, it wasn't me they were after."

Her eyebrows shoot up. "Wow! That's a chunk of money! So what was Kurt's reaction to their loss?"

"I didn't know at the time how much money, of course, but I knew the company drilled some dry holes and the investors weren't happy. I had no idea it was that much until the Attorney General told me." My mouth is really getting dry. "Basically, his reaction to their loss was 'it was business.' Companies lose money all the time. He didn't seem to have any sympathy for them."

Edie senses my discomfort, makes her way to the little refrigerator and holds up a Dr. Pepper, not wanting to interrupt me.

"Sure, thanks, I'd love one. Whenever it came up, he would just say, 'They shouldn't have invested anything they couldn't afford to lose.' I thought that was cold. But I never said so."

The can exhales with a spew. "I love these and you just can't get them in Michigan." She lifts the Dr. Pepper and takes a swig as she hands a second one to me. "What about his biological parents? How'd he find them?"

I start at the beginning, with his memories of another home and family when he was very young and of his mother. How his adoptive mother told him it was all just something he'd dreamed. "Shortly before her death he confronted her with some papers he found, including his old birth certificate and she still couldn't admit that he was adopted. His dad finally told him the truth after her death. Kurt was racked with guilt at the way he treated her because of the memories of torture. He never brought it up with his dad again. Then a few years later, when he was twenty-two, he learned what happened from a female cousin in his adopted mother's family. She told him the adoption was through a family member, a cousin or something in his biological family. He found his birth father in Austin. He was the owner of a night club."

"So he went to see his father?" Edie looks up from her notes.

"Oh yes. He spent a couple of weeks with him. Kurt described him as jovial, like Santa Claus, with a big laugh." I smile when I remember the joy he expressed recalling this happy memory. I open the can and pour the ice-cold drink into a tall, clear glass she'd placed on the table in front of me.

"I can't remember his name." I rub my temple with cold fingers and continue.

"Anyway, his father explained that he and Kurt's mother had divorced soon after Kurt was removed from the home. He and his father became very close. Kurt had a wife and child already —Kacy, his first wife. He began to make plans to move to Austin, but before they could make the move, his father died of a sudden heart attack." I sip the fizzy soda.

"How sad, that must have been a great disappointment." Edie says as she leans in, retrieving her Dr. Pepper, still in the can. "And his mother, where did he find her?"

"This is the really sad part. The wrong parent died. If anyone deserved to die, it was her. He told me that several times. He hated her even more after he met her, old and decrepit, living in a trailer park in Hobbs, New Mexico, with her sixth husband. He told me he wanted to forgive her, but she wouldn't acknowledge she had done anything wrong. She never apologized. He hated her even more after their meeting." I needed Dr. Mann to know the pain and anger he expressed.

"His sister, Melody, he found in Houston, only after pleading with his mother to reveal her whereabouts. She was a speed whore. 'All she wanted from me was money,' he said. He told me she even offered to have sex with him if he would give her money. He was disgusted and returned to Fort Worth. He never saw his mother or sister again, and with his father dead, he put it all behind him and went on with life." I pause, a bubbly sip wetting a mouth that keeps going dry.

"He became a Bible-thumping, judgmental churchgoer. He studied to become a preacher. That's when he and Glynn, my first husband, began to grow apart."

"First? Wait back up." She held up a palm.

"Okay, so my first husband and Kurt were friends since high school. I know it's weird. I married my husband's best friend."

She put pen to paper. "Oh darling, it's not as weird as you think. I've heard it all when it comes to relationships." Looking up, she said, "We may come back to this."

I wipe the sweat from my glass. "Anyway, by the time Kurt and I got together, he'd developed a unique spiritual philosophy."

"Unique? How so?" The notepad rests on her knee as she scribbles, holding the soda can in the opposite hand.

"Well, to me, it was... at the time... uncomfortable, given my Southern Baptist upbringing and all." I find the topic irrelevant. "I'll just say we explored a more universal belief system." I fall silent.

"Well... okay. He sure didn't have much in the way of positive female role models in his life, did he?" she asks rhetorically. "What kind of relationship did he have with his adoptive father?"

"Well it seemed pretty good to me." I tuck a foot up on the sofa under my leg. "At least that's what I thought most of the time I knew him. Jules, his name was Julian but everyone called him Jules, was a quiet man, very sweet, worked hard, but he wasn't timid."

Edie held a finger to her mouth. "What do you mean that's what you thought most of the time?"

"This is strange, and, of course, I didn't understand until years later, but when we announced we were going to get married, Jules caught me alone and said, 'Don't marry Kurt.' I asked why he would say such a thing. And he just repeated,

'Don't marry Kurt.' Then someone came in the room and he never said anything else about it to me." I say it just as it had happened.

"Why do you think he told you that? You said you understood years later. What did you understand him to mean?" She leans back, raises the tip of her index finger to her lip, assuming the analyzing psychologist posture I'd seen in movies.

"Well, Kurt drove me to bankruptcy, he screwed up my life, and maybe the old man was just trying to warn me. Maybe he knew something I didn't."

"Did Kurt ever mention anything in his past about brushes with the law? Or brag about getting away with anything?" She stands and stretches from side to side then massages her lower back.

"I think I understand now why you guys have couches in your offices." I shift my weight to one side and slip a throw pillow under my elbow.

"Hey, make yourself comfortable. We certainly don't need to stand on formality. I want you to remember everything you can about this guy. He's obviously got some issues and the more I learn from you the better chance we have of catching him."

She walks around the sofa and grabs a bag of chips from the mini bar. "Want some?" I wave my hand no.

"Of course, it would be nice if we could locate his third wife." She refers to her notes. "April?"

"Yes, April. That's her name." I shrug. "I have no idea where she is. Last I heard, she was living in Azle with her uncle. Sorry, I don't remember his name."

"Well, she probably couldn't help us much if she's as, well, excuse me, as delicate as you remember her, but I'm sure the police will want to locate her for safekeeping." She wanders back to her seat. "So back to my question, did he ever brag about getting away with anything? Even as a kid?"

I take a deep breath. I do remember some things he'd told me, now that she asks. "He did say he and a friend would take the T-tops off his car and then report them stolen to the insurance company. When I acted surprised by that, he dismissed it. 'Come on everybody does it, and besides, the insurance companies can afford it.' I just let it go. It didn't seem worth the fight.

"One that always bothered me a lot was something he would say when one of his exes would make him mad, really mad. He'd call her a bitch right in front of me and say she'd be better off dead." I put both feet on the floor and look over at Edie.

"Can you believe someone would say something like that? I used to wonder if he'd ever say something like that about me if I made him mad enough." It's late, and I'm getting hungry. "Hey. I have an idea. Let's walk across the street. Do you like steak?" I think she must be getting hungry, also.

"Eating hotel chips isn't exactly dinner is it?" She looks at the bag of chips. "Let's go. I saw the place you're talking about, Del Frisco's?" She points in a generally southern direction.

"Yeah, that's it. But before we go, there is one more thing. It's kind of creepy now that I think about it and looking back now... it might be true," I say with a shiver.

"What?" She places her hand on my arm. I sit back down. "There was a murder a long time ago. I was only eleven or twelve at the time. It was a teenage girl, Dena Morgan. She and her boyfriend were leaving a bowling alley over off the traffic circle, and someone kidnapped her. I think the guy knocked her boyfriend unconscious and took her. I don't really remember much about the details, just that the whole city was looking for her. It was all over the news." I try to remember what Kurt said years later.

"Hap can tell you all about it. I think two weeks later, when they found her in a drainage culvert in Benbrook, he was one of the officers who found her body. They actually questioned Hap, like *he* was a suspect." I stand.

"My mom was so freaked she wouldn't let my sister or me out of the house after dark for months. I don't think they ever found the killer."

"Anyway, Kurt and I were driving past the bowling alley where it happened one day, and he asked me if I remembered the girl that had been murdered, Dena Morgan? He said he went to the same school with her. Then he told me that he was taken in for questioning in that case. He worked at the Dairy Queen down the street from the bowling alley and he wore this big thick, white belt. It seems the boyfriend remembered the assailant wore a wide white belt." I take a deep breath.

"He just laughed because that's all the boyfriend could remember. He never said if he knew her or her boyfriend and he never mentioned it again."

12

*E*die grabs my arm. "Come on, let's go eat." She doesn't act like it's a very big deal. As we walk, I tell her more. "Of course, fat white belts were all the rage back then, along with hip-hugger bell bottoms and big loopy earrings, so it's not like they singled out Kurt for something exceptional. I heard they questioned a lot of men after her disappearance and that they even investigated Hap as a suspect."

It's fairly early on a weekday evening, so we quickly get a table and I order the house Zinfandel. Edie orders a Jack and Diet Coke. "Can't help it, you can take the girl out of Kentucky, but you can't take the Kentucky outta the girl!" She takes a drink and laughs after an accidental burp.

She reminds me of Kathy Bates when she played Evelyn in *Fried Green Tomatoes*. She's very sweet, but a small amount of alcohol encourages a brash, confident woman to speak her mind. "So, did he ever hit you?'

"Oh, God, no, never!"

"Did he ever get angry and threaten to hit you?" Her fore-head wrinkles between her eyebrows.

"No, I mean yes, of course he'd get angry. You know, like I

said, mostly at his son's mothers, and he'd say they'd be better off dead."

"Better off dead? What did you think he meant by that?"

"Just that he wanted them out of his life. He never said he wanted to kill them. I never thought he really wanted them dead, just they'd be better off dead. You know, gone." Remembering his words leaves me feeling anxious.

"So, what do you think now?" She reaches for my hand.

"I wonder, since he's left, if he ever thought that about me, if he ever despised me that much?"

"So is he..." Eddie speaks before I finish the thought.

"I never gave him a reason to hate me, or leave me. I was a good wife. I love... loved him. I still don't know why he left me —me! Not his kids or the possibility of going to jail, but *me*. Why did he leave me?" I look into her eyes, wishing she could give me an answer. She squeezes my hand, affirming my belief she'd like to provide an answer. We sit silent.

"So. was he jealous?"

"No, except once... I had gone to visit my grandmother in Kansas and he called constantly, wanting to know everything we did. He suggested maybe I was going out with someone there. At my grandmother's house, with my sons! I couldn't believe he'd say such a thing to me." My voice becomes louder. I sip the wine, take a deep breath, and calm down. "I was so angry with him. I guess he felt bad for talking to me like that because, when I returned home, he gave me a beautiful gold bracelet with a small two of hearts charm. Which, I discovered later, he charged to *my* credit card." We shake our heads in sync with pursed lips.

"Two of hearts? Was that significant?" she asks.

"Yeah, it was a thing we used to do, like a love note."

"Maybe he was seeing someone while you were out of town, and he felt guilty. You know, like they say, the guilty dog barks first."

"No, I don't think so. I don't want to think so. He was always very attentive." I tell her about the Valentine's Day that I couldn't describe to Sam and Hap.

"Wow!" She's impressed. She gets it.

The waiter places a sumptuous Osso Buco in front of her with flare. It smells delicious and looks like it would melt in your mouth, but the thought of eating veal is not very appetizing to me. He slides my utensils aside with my Carpetbagger rib-eye and Chateau potatoes less ceremoniously. Red meat is not part of my normal diet, and I savor the first bite. Edie hacks away at hers with the enthusiasm of a hungry caveman.

"So, Megan, have you ever thought about what you'd do if he came back? How would you handle that?" Her eyes lock with mine.

It's a test. If I look away, I lose. "Sure, I've thought about it. I've thought about it a lot. How would I handle it?"

She breaks contact first, raises the napkin from her lap, and wipes her mouth. "A rhetorical question, honey, no need to answer."

Is she playing with me?

"I miss Kurt desperately, and I still love him, even after all these years, as crazy as that sounds. Some days, I think if he'd just come back, we could fix it all and I'd have my life back. A normal life, like other people have."

"And then?" The fork pointed at me mimics her serious tone.

"Then, what?" *What does she want from me?*

"The other days? You said *some days* you think, if he came back, you could fix it and move on. What about the other days? How do you feel those days?"

"Oh... on those days... honestly?" A twirl of her fork indicates 'yes, honest answer please.'

"Well of course it's an impossibility now, given what's happened." The controlled demeanor I've maintained slowly drains from every pore, bathing me with a familiar anger.

"I'd like to see him suffer. Slowly. How would you feel if you were me?" Maybe she'll tell me how I should've responded to her question.

"Me? Let's see I'd string him up by his balls and cut his tongue out. I'd make sure the son-of-a-bitch paid for screwing me over!" Edie stuffs an oversized piece of meat in her mouth. I've lost my appetite and push the remaining food around on the plate before emptying my wine glass.

"Now, about his first marriage," she gurgles while chewing. Not very ladylike at all. "Can you tell me what it was like?"

I fill her in about how we used to hang out together playing cards and all, but explain that in the early days I was really closer to Kacy than I was to Kurt. I heard the highlights in their lives but the part about him finding his parents must have escaped me at the time, because I didn't remember it at all.

"I was busy with my kids and alcoholic, wanna be rock-star husband, and believe me, that was exhausting!"

She shifts in her chair and pulls the tablecloth with her. "Especially at such a young age. You know what they say— that's why God gives 'em to the young." Her teeth pull the rare meat, and she chews vigorously.

"Sounds like *that* husband of yours was more of a kid than your boys." I toast her statement and nod my head.

"Amen sister, you got it! Now, he's another woman's problem."

Wedging a gold American Express Card into the check binder, she declares, "It's business, I've got it." She waves my hand away.

We head back across the street and I stop to light a cigarette in front of the hotel. Edie motions for one. I hand one to her and hold up the lighter, shielding the flame from the wind that kicked up since we went into the restaurant. She takes a long, slow drag.

"Oh, I miss these." She says. "I'm wondering, and I have to ask, what happened with all that money?"

I stash the pack back into my purse. "I don't really know. I don't think he had any or much of any when he left. I'm sure it was used to meet payroll for the companies. He did receive bonuses though, nice bonuses."

I stretch my neck and take another puff. There's something about alcohol and nicotine. They go hand-in-hand, and I crave another drink.

As I stamp out both butts with the tippy toe of my shoe, Edie locks elbows with me and proclaims, "We're going to the bar. This hotel has a nice one." We get comfortable in a booth far from the sports on the television, and she locates a pad and pen from her oversized hobo Dooney & Bourke.

"Let's see, you asked about the money." I figure I might as well tell her of our travels. "One day, outta the blue, he called and told me to go to the post office and pick up two passport applications. I did, and he sent off our applications the next day, with pictures from the JC Penney's photo shop. Only after they were in the mail did he tell me he had bought two tickets to London." I take a sip from a glass of a red wine I didn't order.

"The gentlemen over there bought you women a round of drinks." A rotund waiter points to two old men sitting at the end of the bar. I'm disgusted at the sight of them. They're old enough to be my father.

"How nice!" Edie exclaims, tossing a polite but noncommittal toast in their direction. "Salud, thank you!" She turns her attention back to me. "So, you went to London? That must have been fun?"

"Yeah, it was. We saw the changing of the guards at Buckingham Palace and rode the Tube. We took the train to the white cliffs of Dover, toured the castle and rode the Hovercraft over the English Channel to Calais. You know in France?" She peers over her shoulder at the old coots.

"Yeah, yeah... I've heard. I've never been, but I've seen pictures of those places. Lucky you... someday I'm going." She pats my hand and pulls a cigarette from my pack on the table.

"Oh, that's not all. We drove up to Oxford and on to the

Cotswolds. He had some business to tend to, and I spent a couple of days in a fairy tale of a town, so wide-eyed and innocent. I felt like a child, but he seemed to fit right in. It was odd."

I'm feeling kind of immature and giddy now, reliving it all in front of her. She appears preoccupied. "There's more," I continue. "You asked."

We laugh. "Okay, give it to me, girl! What a life you've had."

I go on. "Well, I guess now that I think about it, I do know where a lot of the money went. We traveled a lot. After London, we went to Acapulco." The thought brings the smell of burning trash to mind. Every morning, smoke rose on the horizon. "We saw the cliff divers, you know like in the old Elvis movie?"

Edie nods. "*Fun in Acapulco,* I loved that movie. God! I miss Elvis," she says with a whiny voice. She's drunk.

"We saw where it was filmed and rode horses on the beach close to where one of the Rambo movies was filmed. Gushing with memories of visions, tastes, and odors I tell her of the food.

"We ate coconut shrimp and drank far too many Coronas under a thatched roof."

Lost in thought, I hear Steve Winwood's *Shadows in Purple* from the large black speakers suspended from the grassy ceiling. "It was warm and peaceful. I have seen some beautiful places." The melody plays in my head. I sang along to the lyrics of the song that day, unaware in a few short weeks the anguish in those words would be thrust upon me as I cried myself awake every night.

"Was he just crazy about Rambo?" she interrupts my thoughts.

"Oh no, I don't think so. Why? Does that mean something?" I remember why we're talking about all this in the first place.

She scrawls long words. "So, was he a movie buff?"

"No, it just seems that I remember the trivia from our trips. You know, places I saw in the movies as a kid. Places I never thought I'd visit. I feel like such a child sometimes, always wanting to see and do. My mom says I was even afraid to sleep because I might miss something."

"What about your dad, Megan? What kind of relationship do you and your dad have?"

"I don't." There's not enough alcohol in this entire bar to make me talk about my father. "It's getting late, and I think the tales of my adventures have worn us both out."

"You don't have a relationship with him?"

"No, he left us when I was a kid." I lift the pack of cigarettes from the table and place them in my purse.

"Being abandoned once is hard enough, but twice? Most people would… well never mind." Edie puts her hand on top of mine when I reached for the lighter. "Where's your father now?"

"I don't know. I mean, I know I could find him if I needed to. Listen, it's late, and I really should get home. My poor dogs…" I pull my hand from under hers.

"Yeah, you're right, it is getting late. Megan? I have one more question. Why?"

I stand to leave. "Why, what?"

As she stands one of the men calls out. "Ah ladies, where ya going? The night's still young!"

Yeah, but you're not. You're old and decrepit.

"Why would Kurt come back and murder these women? He successfully disappears for six years and he's just gonna come to murder two women. Why?" Edie digs in the monstrous bag as we walk toward the elevator. "Ah ha!" She holds up her room key.

I dig deep, but don't have an answer for her. "Uh…"

"It was another rhetorical question, Hon. How could anyone but Kurt know the answer to that, huh? Listen, it sure was nice to meet you. I've had an enjoyable day. Not like work at all."

"Well, if you're ever down this way again, we should get together."

"Yes, I think we should. I leave tomorrow, but depending

how this progresses, I'd like to continue where we left off, sometime soon." She pats my arm, closes her notebook, and stuffs it in her purse. "Oh! I left my pen on the table. Now you drive careful." She takes off toward the bar, the gauzy material of her skirt flowing behind her.

The trip to Oklahoma City was a nice break from the routine. After my return, the days seem to drag by with no word on Missy's or Kacy's deaths. I don't pry into the investigation or ask questions regarding any aspect of the cases. I just mind my casework, mostly drugs. Dirty syringes containing bloody residue and small plastic baggies of powder make me wonder how people plunge the stuff into their veins and up their noses. Some days I wonder what keeps me from doing the same. How did my life stray so far from the simple plans I had for us? Without the tug of responsibility to my boys, maybe I'd be an addict too.

The holiday season always brings a flurry of suicide and domestic violence scenes. I know I'll be busy, but being single and the thought of the boys being away for Christmas depresses me. I find my escape, although short-lived, in alcohol. It numbs the pain and takes away the fear.

∽

12:00 A.M., Friday, November 18, 1994

A noise outside my bedroom window jerks me awake. The

dogs sit up on the bed, but they don't bark. Startled, I wonder did I really hear something or dream it. The glass of wine I'd had before dinner relaxed me, and I was in a deep sleep. Maybe it was something on the TV. I reach for the remote and click off the noise. We stare at the window and listen intently. Alpha jumps down. Standing in front of the window, his fur on end, he growls in a low tone. He raises his nose and sniffs the air with quick puffs. Beta sits still between me and the window. Neither barks. There we sit, frozen. Slowly, I grope for the piece of paper with Hap's number I'd placed beside the phone just in case. My hands shake. The numbers beep loudly as I press them. Alpha remains in his guarded stance by the window.

"Hello." A gruff sleepy answer.

"Hap?" I whisper.

"Yes, yes… Megan?" he says, recognizing my voice.

"Someone is outside my bedroom window." My quiet voice alarms him.

"Get your gun and stay right where you are. I'm on my way." Click, the dial tone returns. I'm paralyzed. Gun? I don't own a gun. I wait what seems like an eternity. He lives only minutes away. I lay back, feel my heart fluttering, and try to decide what we heard. Was it the wind or maybe a garden tool fell? Just then, a shadow passes the window. The pounding in my chest reaches my ears.

Bang, bang, bang! My heart races again. Someone is at the back door in the den. I jump from the bed trying not to trip on the dogs. They run barking. As I cautiously walk through the dark house, I reason that it's probably Connor. He'd gone to a freshman basketball game and most likely forgotten his keys. The dogs jump on the door, barking wildly. If it's Connor why are they so agitated? A stranger surely wouldn't want this much attention. I flick the light switch. *Damn, the bulb's burned out!*

Instinctively, I turn the bolt-lock, "Connor?" In that split-second, I realize my mistake as the door is pushed open, causing me to stumble backward and trip over Beta. Before I land, she skitters away yelping, and Alpha runs for the kitchen, to hide. Beta returns to stand her ground and protect us. She bares her teeth and growls at the intruder. By the time I realize it's not Connor, it's too late. In the darkness, a tall figure reaches down for me. Scooting back on palms and heels, I look up and can't see a face. Beta unleashes her anger, tearing fabric as she yanks on a pant leg aggressively. A hand grabs my arm yanking me up toward him.

Hap's voice scolds me. "What the hell are you doing? Let me help you up!" He shakes free of Beta and inspects his torn trousers.

Breathless and shaking, I strike his chest. "I didn't know it was you. You scared me!"

"Then why the hell did you open the door?" The chastising continues.

"I thought Connor forgot his key again," I say, justifying my actions. "Why are you at the back door?"

Beta's at my side, ready to reengage if necessary. "It's okay Beta! Good Girl!" I praise her heroic behavior.

"I walked around the house. A screen is off back there." He points his flashlight to the back of the house. "Is that where your bedroom is? Back that way?"

"Oh my God!" In disbelief, I grasp my head in both hands, in an effort to stop the sound of my pounding heart there.

"Where's your gun?" He lays a hand on my shoulder, and Beta growls again.

Reminded of her brother, I walk into the kitchen to check on Alpha. He's cowering in the corner presenting a submissive posture as I approach. "It's okay, Baby, everything's fine." I reassure and rub behind his ear. "I don't have a gun!" I reply with a defensive chuckle. "With kids in the house all the time? Are you crazy? Don't you think that's a little risky? Just how many juvenile accidental shooting scenes have we worked?" I yell, and with an arc of my wrists, display my faithful companions parked on either side. "And I have these two for protection."

"Well, they make a good alarm, but this settles it. I'm assigning an officer to you around the clock, starting tomorrow." He lifts the trimline phone from the wall and pokes at the buttons, stretching the tangled cord to find a comfortable leaning spot. I snatch it from him.

He reaches for it, and I hide it behind my back. "No! I don't want someone watching me twenty-four hours a day. We'll be just fine." He slowly walks to me, reaches around my back, and places his large hand on mine holding the phone. Pulling me close to him, I bury my head in his chest, relieved. He pries the phone from my defiant grip.

"It's okay! Don't worry, I'll protect you." Hap wraps me in his arms and I cry. He pats the back of my head, smoothing my hair. "What do ya have to drink? I think you need something to calm your nerves." He puts a finger under my chin, raises my face to his. Kissing my forehead, he pushes my shoulders back, forcing me away from him.

Looking me in the eyes, he waits for an answer. "Yeah, sure, what do you want?" I wipe the tears from my cheeks and pull my hair up and back, then let it fall. Without a robe, I now feel a bit naked. I seek shelter in the pantry.

Peering around the refrigerator he watches me tiptoe and burrow through items on a high shelf. "What are you doing?"

"I have to hide any liquor I buy, because the boys and their friends will drink it." Struggling, I push a stack of cookbooks aside and seize the object. "I know you don't have kids, but you were a teenager once weren't you?"

Jim Beam in hand, I instruct him to the glasses in the cabinet near the sink. I plunk a couple of ice cubes in each, pour the whiskey, and add about a tablespoon of water to his. That's how he always orders it. Hap sits facing me as I step into the den. Back-lighting from the kitchen must be projecting the silhouette of my figure beneath my thin gown. I catch him staring at me and notice a flush redness on his cheeks.

"Congratulations on making Lieutenant, Lieutenant Parks."

Walking toward him I raise my shot of whiskey and hand him a glass.

"Thanks." He takes the glasses from me and places them on the coffee table then grabs my hands in his with a squeeze.

"Are you okay?" I ask, looking down at him, and with a quick squeeze back, I break contact with him.

"No, I'm not Megan. I'm worried about you! You act like you're not upset by all of this bullshit, but you need to be. This is serious. He's already killed twice. Don't you realize you could be next?" The tone of his voice starts soft, yet grows increasingly louder.

In the kitchen, I rummage through random drawers for an old pack of smokes. Once located, I flick on a gas burner, situate a cigarette between my lips, and remove my hair from harm's way. "Why would he hurt me? I never did anything to him. He's the one who left me."

I draw a stale breath from it and take a gulp of the Jim Beam. Hap steals the cigarette from me and puffs. I frown and confiscate it. "You are not going to start that again."

He clenches my wrist and with a twist, pulls me close to him again. I resist. He teasingly pulls harder. I lose my balance and fall into him against the counter, surprising both of us. I lean my head back, look into the steel blue eyes. Just at the moment when this relationship could change forever, thumping music from the car of Connor's ride rattles the house. I jump up and run quickly to get my robe.

As I make it back to the den, Connor's coming in the door. "Hey! Hap, what's up?"

"Hey! Big guy, how ya doing?" Hap lifts from the sofa and they shake hands.

I look at my watchless wrist and then at Connor.

"I know I'm late, but we had to take Michael home, and his dad wanted to show us his new computer. I swear!"

My doubtful squint prompts a declaration of truth from him. "Honest, Mom! You can call him."

He turns his back and heads quickly for the stairs. "Goodnight!" A foot lands on every other step, and he's out of sight.

"There's no logic to what Kurt's doing, Megan," Hap picks right up. "He has a twisted view of women. The report we got from Dr. Mann confirms it—he's a psycho. The lack of sexual assaults on these women exhibits such intense anger, not power or control, but a deep-seated anger. Dr. Mann's theory is that this is not a crime against women, but *the* women in his life that never fulfilled the love and acceptance he didn't receive from his biological mother." He swirls the final swallow of bourbon around in the glass. "According to Dr. Mann, it goes back to his childhood. Hell, that sister of his was really something."

I wonder if she mentioned my telling her Kurt and Hap were questioned in Dena Morgan's murder. I hope not—surely not, that wouldn't be professional. He downs the last of the whiskey while walking to the kitchen, dumps the ice in the sink, and sets the glass beside it.

"I'll be sending someone tomorrow." He reclaims his flashlight from the counter top.

"No, Hap, please!" I beg. "I don't want anyone watching my house and following me around!"

He turns the bolt lock on the back door and heads for the front. "Oh, I'm going to do better than that. I'm sending a female officer here to stay with you and Connor. One with a gun."

He opens the front door and makes a hasty retreat before I can protest further. "Lock the door! See you tomorrow," he says, waving his hand overhead as he struts toward his car.

At 2:00 a.m. I head back to my now-cold bed, throttling the bottle of Jim Beam. How I would love someone warm to cuddle next to the remainder of the night. Telepathic Alpha jumps up on the bed, his sister following. They each assume their spot, providing warmth, and we settle in for the duration.

*a*t 6:00 a.m., the doorbell rings and I grab my robe, preparing myself for just about anything. I open the door and there stands Jackie, suitcase in hand. An overloaded backpack is slung over one shoulder. Connor approaches, rubbing his eyes.

"Jackie?" I shield my eyes from the bright sunrise. "What are you doing here?"

She looks at me with her doe-like violet eyes and turns her head, then motions to the white Ford sedan in the street parked behind her car, a blue Jeep Cherokee. Hap waves.

"He's been here all night." She flings her backpack on the tile floor and heaves the suitcase in my direction. It's almost as big as she is.

The sight brings a familiar voice to mind. *'She's no bigger'n a pound 'a soap after a day's washing!'* My Grannie had a saying for just about every observation in life.

"He looks terrible, didn't get an ounce of sleep. I'm surprised he didn't just call for a patrol car to do the job." She bobs to one side, and I block her.

"We really don't need you to stay here."

"You tell Hap." She pushes me aside and walks in.

I introduce the new housemates. "Connor, this is Jackie. Jackie, Connor." Peering through the decreasing crack in the door I see Hap pull from the curb. A curious neighbor waves and spills his coffee while bending to collect the paper.

"Jackie Taylor," Jackie says as she reaches for Connor's hand. Now fully alert, he shakes her hand and takes the cumbersome luggage.

"I'll put this up in Ian's room, Mom. She can stay there. He won't mind."

If it was an ugly old guy, I suspect he would not be so accommodating.

"Come on up. I'll show you where your new digs are." He grabs her backpack and lumbers up the stairs. "Would you like some coffee or something?" In his most grownup voice, he hollers down at me. "Mom! Are you gonna make coffee? I think we could all use some."

"Good Morning, America!" the TV shouts as I turn it on and trudge toward the kitchen. Connor doesn't even know why she's here, but he couldn't be happier.

"Well, I showed her the bathroom and gave her some fresh sheets," he says after returning downstairs.

"That's good, thanks honey." I rub his back.

"Mom, is she a friend of yours or something? Who is she? Why did Hap spend the night out there in his car?"

Now I'm going to have to drudge up old memories with Connor. He was very fond of Kurt, but a bit young to understand the details when he left.

"Connor, we need to talk. Why don't you take the bus down to the lab when school lets out today? Okay?" I pour a cup of coffee for each of us and get the cream out of the refrigerator.

"Mom, what's wrong? I knew something was up. Why was Hap here last night?" Confusion crosses his young face. In the background, the television updates the nation on the current time and temperature.

"Just come and see me after school. I'll tell you all about it, okay?" I pat him on the shoulder and squeeze his neck. He ducks, knowing my next move is to rub his head.

"The bus? Man... I can't wait 'til I have a car. Well okay, if it means she's gonna be living here, it can't be all that bad," he whispers, pointing at the ceiling, then pops a grape in his mouth.

"Go on now, times a wastin'. Get ready for school," Connor broadcasts in singsong to Jackie as he stomps up the stairs.

"Jackie, coffee's ready!"

Jackie reappears and perches on a barstool. I tear an English muffin in half and place it in the toaster. We go through the household routine and occupants, starting with the dogs parked at my feet.

"The big one is Alpha and the little one is his sister, Beta." Then I move on to Connor. "He's in the tenth grade at Brewer High School and I'm sure he will tell you, if he hasn't already, he just got his learner's permit to drive. Please, don't feel obligated in any way to let him drive your car." The muffin pops up with a ding. I plop it on a plate, pushing it and the butter dish toward her. "I've been scared for him to drive since he learned how to ride a bicycle. He's such a daredevil. He was only nine when Kurt left. I think he still has difficulty accepting it."

"I would have never thought that you'd have a kid that old. You certainly don't look it!"

"Yeah, well thanks, I started young."

"Ian is a freshman at Florida State on a basketball scholarship. He'll be nineteen next month. I still can't believe how the years have gone so fast. He's tall, blond, and incredibly smart." I raise my hand in the air to indicate how tall. "I have no fears for him. The hand of God always seems to rescue him. Don't get me wrong, he's a good kid. He just always comes out the shining star. I'm glad he doesn't yet understand he has the world by the tail."

"You beam when you talk of your boys. You must be very proud." She eats the last bite of muffin. "I can't wait to be a mom. I've always wanted children, and my biological clock is ticking." She taps her foot several times on the floor mimicking a character's action in a recent comedy. "Too bad the only guys I meet are losers or cops—or both!"

"I hear ya!" I nod and we laugh in harmony. With a serious tone, Jackie explains her urgency for children.

"My mom is very sick. She has ovarian cancer. My dad takes good care of her, but the doctors don't give us much hope. I'd love to give her a grandchild before she dies." I don't mention it, but I wonder if ovarian cancer is hereditary.

MARYJO CRACKS the door to the lab and leans in. "I signed your kid in and took him to your office. Ya might wanna get to him before Sam finds him unaccompanied."

I find Connor spinning around in my chair. A propulsion kick at my desk every couple of turns keeps up his momentum. When he sees me, he blurts out, "Man, I can't wait 'til I have a cushy job like this, making big bucks."

Successfully concealing his unsupervised moments in the crime lab, I shut the door. "Yeah, yeah, get outta my chair, Einstein!" Shooing him away from my desk, I direct him to a seat in the corner, filled with clutter. He unloads the chair and pulls it up to the desk. With both elbows on the desk, he quips, "Okay, what's up?"

"I think you've heard about Kacy's death?" He nods.

"And there's been another death. Missy. You remember her, don't you?" I try to read his face.

"Yeah, Matthew's mom. She died, too?" He is very surprised. "On the news, they said Kacy killed herself, didn't she? They're both dead. Wow! That's weird." I can see he's putting it together. "How did Missy die?"

"She was found in her garage. She died of asphyxia." I simplify. "Carbon monoxide poisoning. Her car was left running and she died from the fumes. But, it may have been set up to look like a suicide."

Connor is an intelligent kid, and it doesn't take long for the summation. "Is it Kurt? Did he kill them?"

Before I can answer he's on his feet. "That's why Jackie's at the house! She's a cop! Okay, okay, I get it now. It all makes sense. They think Kurt did it and you're next. No wait!" He stops. "That crazy lady would be next, if he's going in order. What was her name?"

"April," I answer. "We don't know anything right now. It could just be a coincidence." I try to curb his fears.

"Mom! You need to be careful. Maybe he's gone crazy, too!"

"Connor, Connor, slow down, honey. It's all just speculation right now." His anxiety level seems to be increasing with each progressive thought. Scratching his head, he paces in front of the desk.

"Oh my God, Mom. You're in real danger! That's why Hap was at the house last night when I got home, isn't it?" He leans into the window and looks down at the street. "Man, I thought y'all were having a thing or something." His breath fogs the glass.

"Connor!" I gasp.

"Well, that's what it looked like to me!" Arms crossed, he defends the statement.

"He's married!"

"So, you're not."

"Alright, that's enough." My patience is wearing thin with this topic. "Anyway, I wanted you to know why Jackie is going to be staying with us. Hap insists."

"I think it's great. I can't wait for Michael to see her. She's a babe, a real hottie." He puffs up, like he's just been awarded the virility badge.

"Leave her alone. You know she's almost twice your age," I say, lying. I can almost hear cogs grinding and gears clicking as I see his thoughts quickly turn to telling the news to his best friend. He grows restless.

"I gotta go, I've got lots of homework!" Slinging the shabby backpack over one shoulder, he darts out the door.

I'd never seen such enthusiasm about homework before, real or imagined. "Well, get home and get to it!" I shout to his disappearing back, knowing Jackie is in her office and not at the house.

I return home with extra keys for Jackie and takeout Kentucky Fried honey barbecued chicken for the three of us, mine and Connor's new junk food favorite. I hope Jackie approves. She isn't here, and Connor seems disappointed. As I peel my clothes off and seriously consider a nice hot bath before messy chicken in front of the TV, a knock at my bedroom door hinders the thought. I open the door to find Jackie raising a fist to knock again. "You were supposed to wait at the lab... until I show up to follow you home. You're gonna get me fired. Hap will put me back on patrol, or worse, back in that vacuum of economic crime nerds, if I can't keep up with you!" She looks pissed.

"I'm sorry. I didn't realize I couldn't drive home alone. You want to come watch me take a bath?" Standing in my bra and panties, I try to bring a little humor to the moment.

Jackie doesn't think it's funny. "You think I'm lesbian, don't you? Because I'm a cop. Everyone thinks women cops are lesbians."

I can't help myself, I burst out laughing. I laugh so hard it brings tears to my eyes.

"Lesbian?" Connor says. I close the door enough to conceal my state of undress. "You? You're a lesbian?" he says with a mixture of disbelief and grief.

"No. I'm not!" When she turns and sees the look on Connor's face, she begins laughing herself.

Connor looks confused. He caught the tail-end of what she had said to me, and I was laughing so hard I couldn't talk. Just the thought of someone as petite, foo-fooey, and feminine as her being gay struck me as funny. I spent years with a lesbian sister who is no lipstick lesbian but definitely less butch than a hard-core female athlete. I have gaydar, and Jackie is definitely at the far end of that spectrum.

Our shared ice-breaking moment makes for an easy evening, and we eat our dinner at the dining table for a change. She reassures Connor that she is not a lesbian, and he teases her. "Hey, really it's okay if you are. My aunt Tara is gay. She's great, you'll like her. Mom, let's fix 'em up." Jackie slaps his shoulder and smiles.

THE NEXT MORNING as we head out for work, I hand her keys to the house, but I don't reveal I had them made on the way home from work yesterday during a forbidden, unscheduled stop.

15

MONDAY, JANUARY 23, 1995

"*S*top it, you're gonna make me have a wreck!" I joke around with Connor as we fight over radio choices. Each of us pushes buttons for our preset stations, canceling the previous selection. "Hey, driver rules!" I remind him.

"Okay. Then let me drive." He flashes a toothy grin.

Our taste in music is completely opposite. He prefers bebop-ping rapper shit with a bass so hard it vibrates the rear-view mirror, and I prefer country. After surviving the holidays unscathed, we make our annual trek to the Fort Worth Fat Stock Show and Rodeo. We rarely attend the rodeo, but we like to go see the livestock and new gadgets in the exhibit halls. His closest friend, Michael, is joining us again this year. Connor's known Michael since his family moved to our neighborhood about ten years ago. Michael is a year younger than Connor. I thought once school started, they'd drift apart, but they didn't.

Connor and Michael burst out of the car, kicking dirt up in the cold breeze. "Come on, come on," Connor nags, rushing me.

"Alright already! I'm coming!" Zipping up the short rabbit-fur jacket, I swing my heavy purse over a shoulder and slam the car door. "I know you're ready to get to the midway, ride the rides, and flirt with girls," I joke with them. "That's what I used to do with my free ticket and the day out of school for the stock show."

They both giggle and look at me. "You...?" Michael blurts.

I quickly cut him off. "Except it was boys—I flirted with the boys." Connor reaches for Michael's cap and pulls it down over his eyes. "Hey!" They slap at each other, and Connor wins as Michael darts away. The midway was the first place I smoked a cigarette. My junior high school friends and I thought we looked sophisticated. I wonder what behaviors Connor has already developed that I know nothing of. Although I never smoke around him, surely he knows, and hopefully he won't pick up this bad habit. The boys hand over their tickets to the gatekeeper and wait while I buy mine and walk through. Michael whispers something to Connor.

"Mom can you give me ten bucks?" Connor relays the request.

"You have money."

"Just in case?" He puts his palms together in mock prayer. "Pleeease! I won't spend it, unless we have to."

I exhume my freshly buried wallet from its nice resting place in my purse. "All I have is a twenty." Displaying it pinched between finger and thumb.

"Even better!" His eyes light up as he grabs it from my hand.

"Hey!" I reach out, trying to snatch it back from him.

"You owe me!" They take off in a jog toward the carnival rides. "Maybe a clean garage is in order? Be back here at three o'clock," I holler and point to the ground. "Right here—at three."

"Alright, three, got it. We'll be here—at three." They disappear in the crowd, slapping each other on the back, their laughter visible in the winter sun.

It's a beautiful sunny day. The stock show is famous for having the most predictable of the unpredictable Texas weather. It will turn wet and even colder before the annual event concludes in a few days. Two days ago, the wind chill was fourteen below zero. Fortunately for me, I was inside all day, holding my breath. Last week a four-year-old girl was abducted. We're all hoping she'll be found alive and well, but it doesn't look good. It's not a parental abduction. Her bones will probably be found years from now, accidentally, by someone riding their horse in the woods.

Alone, and killing time, I make my way out of the bright daylight and brittle cold wind into the main exhibit hall. I enjoy meandering the aisles aimlessly, looking at farm equipment I'll never need, the "Amazing!" Ginzu knife, and toddlers in strollers. The smell of funnel cakes and sausages makes me think of how many miles of running it would take to burn off one indulgent treat. Racks and racks of color catch my eye at the Justin boot exhibit. The tourists are buying, but most locals know to go to the Justin outlet on Vickery and pay half the price they're charging here. After all the visual stimulation, I look at the big clock, 1:30. I remember a friend of Glynn's used to say any time after noon was beer-thirty, so I walk through the breezeway to the Round-up Inn. It's not an inn, actually, but a hall. I've attended numerous charity balls and fundraising events in the big room, sometimes on Hap's arm, sometimes with a group of coworkers, but never alone. As I enter, I feel eyes on me. Twangy country music explodes from a corner stage as the Dixie Chicks belt out *Sin Wagon*. Being tall and blonde always draws attention. My refuge is the bar in the far corner. The saddle-shaped bar stool is too heavy for me to move and merely rocks as I try. Natalie sings, of the Lord and gettin' ammunition. The bartender wipes up a spill and looks at me with a 'what'll you have' face. "I'll have a Shiner." She brings the sweating bottle and wraps it with a napkin.

"That'll be three-fifty." *Three-fifty?*

I pay and look past her as a vision appears in the mirror behind the bar. It's a glimpse of the past, a happy couple holding hands—Kurt as crisp as a cracker in his starched jeans and button-up Oxford shirt, me wearing the tight, high-waist Rockies that define my pear-shaped hips and enhance my small waist.

As we make our way through the crowd, we see people whisper and stare, every woman wishing she were me and every man wishing he were Kurt.

I shake the thought from my head and turn to face the expansive room. The memory of how festive it appeared for the Margarita Ball last month surfaced. Enormous Christmas trees filled every corner. Donated toys and bicycles brought by partiers in formal attire adorned every inch around the tree bases, quite a contrast to the jeans and sweaters worn by moms and dads pushing kids in strollers today. The long white tables no longer draped in green linen are sporadically occupied and littered with Styrofoam plates holding the leftover remnants of dinner from Coburn's Bar-B-Que buffet line along the northwest corner.

My eye catches a familiar figure. His gait is unforgettable, shoulders back and posture perfect. The crisp, starched, pink button-down shirt and pressed jeans send a hot flush up my neck and into my cheeks. It wasn't just a memory in the mirror. I think I see Kurt at the far side of the room, longneck bottle in hand, walking arm in arm with a very thin, skanky blond. Maintaining my composure, I pick up my beer and follow at a distance, but I doubt myself for a moment. For many months after he left, I thought I saw him everywhere, only to be disappointed when I got close enough to see that it wasn't him. They approach the row of metal doors, and he pushes the release bar on one and holds it open. I notice the grey streak in his hair. It's him! I stand paralyzed as people rush all around me.

A cold wind blows against them. She turns, chasing the sleeve of a puffy red jacket with her left hand. Kurt jostles, holding the door for others and helping her. A gust of wind blows the hair away from her face. That's when I see it's April. I walk at an angle out of his view to a door at the far end. Opening it slowly, I peer out. At the edge of the steps, I see them headed for the parking lot. Frozen, I watch as they weave through the sea of pickup trucks and sedans. Her long hair whips in the wind as they lengthen their stride and run out of sight.

Numbness sets in as my entire body shakes. I grip the neck of the bottle, and the thought of a well-aimed pitch that clips Kurt's head gives me warmth. I need a cigarette to go with the beer I don't chunk. I gather the fur collar up under my chin and walk quickly to the small livestock barns where I know I can smoke out of the cold. The odor of urine burns my nostrils as I tug the door open. The smell should certainly cancel the odor of smoke, so no one will care. I sit at a small table covered with red checked plastic, cigarette in an unsteady hand, and dig for a lighter in my disorganized purse. I can't collect my thoughts, not sure what to do. A flame appears at the end of a man's arm from behind me.

"Well, look what the wind blew in." The deep sarcastic drawl sobers me.

Hap grabs a flimsy metal chair and straddles it. His large frame in the small chair looks comical. Our knees touch and neither one of us withdraws.

"What the hell are you doing here?"

The first drag calms me. "Just looking for a light. Thanks." I blow a cloudy breath over our heads. "And you've rescued me again."

"Where is Jackie? And why are you shaking?" He rubs my thigh.

"You know her mom's pretty sick, and she wanted Jackie to go with her to the doctor today. So, I decided to come with Connor and his friend today. She knew I wouldn't be alone. And I'm shaking because it's cold in here. If you hadn't noticed."

Hap leans forward, putting weight on my leg and turns his head up and down the corridor of the barn. "And they are… where?"

"They're at the midway for a while. I'm meeting them at three… at the gate." I point west.

He stares at me, a good scolding on the tip of his tongue, but not knowing what to say, he extricates himself from the chair and stands tall. "Alright, but I swear, I'm gonna have a talk with that girl about what duty is."

"For crying out loud, Hap! It's her mom! I'd do the same thing. Family's family!" I notice a uniformed cop coming up behind him.

"Hap!" A palm lands on his back with a start. "Hey, Lieutenant! How are ya?"

"Charlie! So this is where they've been hiding you. I haven't seen you since..." Hap extends his hand and plants the other on Charlie's shoulder as they shake.

"Since Laura's wedding," he finishes Hap's sentence for him. "And that's been four years now. We have a grandson now, and she's expecting another any day." Charlie's shirt is stretched tight over his protective vest. Static crackles on his radio, *Ten-thirty-seven, quadrant three.* He clicks the receiver on his shoulder, leans into it and responds. "Ten-four. Hap, duty calls. We've gotta get together real soon, it's been way too long."

"Yea, Charlie it has. Give that beautiful wife of yours a kiss for me. I'll call ya." Hap cups his bicep with another handshake. "And lay off the barbells will ya? You're making the rest of us old guys look bad!"

He turns his attention back to me. "Okay, well, I need to go over to the horse barns. There's a couple-a fillies I wanna bid on. Wanna go?"

"Oh no, it's after two now." I check my watch. "I'll just stick around here 'til I meet the boys."

Hap looks relieved and the promise of a quick departure halts any chance I might have had to overcome my hesitation and tell him what I witnessed. I adjust my watch and throw the cigarette to the dirty concrete floor, stamping it out with my boot.

"I'll wait right here. I swear." I hold up my right hand. "Couldn't be safer."

He places his hand on top of my head, a spark of static making him flinch.

"Always knew there was electricity between us." He winks.

I look up at him and swat at a couple of long hairs trying to follow his hand. He reminds me of all the good in Kurt, perhaps because they are both Libras.

"Before you leave, can ya light me up one more time?" Hap produces his lighter and obliges my request.

"I'm calling this evening. We're not done here." He shuffles off to the horse barns.

Contemplating another beer, I remember the bottle of whiskey secreted under my bed. I wait in the vestibule for a sheltered but clear view of Connor and Michael's return. I meet them as they arrive, and we proceed to the car. "Mom! You smell like cigarettes, yuck!"

Once home, I offer to cook dinner. He rubs his belly. "You know that twenty you gave me? We ate it up." Off the hook, I retreat to the privacy of my room. My fingertips feel for the bottle. It rolls just beyond my reach and rests next to the little box of trinkets. If I imagine hard enough, I can hear my Daddy saying, *Magpie, my clever little bird.* I caress the carving, sit cross-legged on the floor, and inspect the treasures that comingle my past and present. The alcohol burns my throat with the first swig. From the pile, I untangle a gold bracelet with one charm, the two of hearts. The inventory includes two seashells, an arrowhead, a crystal shard, a prized barrette stolen from Tara, Connor's first lost tooth, the bracelet, two small green glass beads in the corner, and a brass key stamped 3717 wrapped in paper. I've contemplated returning Tara's barrette since I was twelve. Since I found the bundle of paper behind the TV set six months ago, I've wondered what lock the key opens and the significance of the paper.

The next morning, as we make our way to our vehicles with my head throbbing, I extend an invitation to Jackie. "My brother called and would like to take us all fishing Saturday morning if the weather's nice. Are you up for it?"

"Yeah, sounds like fun. Hey, don't drive so fast. It's hard for me to keep up," Jackie yells as I nod my head in agreement through the closed window.

I roll it down. "I just forget you're following me. Sorry."

16

FEBRUARY 12, 1995

*E*arly Saturday morning, I find Connor stacking gear by the door and rummaging through his tackle box on the dining table.

"Hey, can we have a clean spot for breakfast?" I demand and push the box to the edge of the table with a plate.

He gathers all of his own fishing equipment and proudly proclaims he's made a basic kit for Jackie from Ian's neatly organized supply. If Ian knew anything had been removed from his designated storage area in the garage, he'd be upset, but I was sure after Connor explained, Ian would make an exception and be more upset at Connor's good fortune.

For an early morning in February, it's nice and sunny. "The weather man says we might get up to 70 degrees today," Connor muffles through shoveled pancakes.

Edward and James are every boy's dream uncles. Over the years, Edward became Ed and that was okay, but never Eddie, and James never converted to a Jim. Connor and Ian are like the sons that neither of them had. They are good men. I want my boys to spend as much time as possible with my brothers. Hopefully, they'll be more like their uncles than their father. With Ian away at school, Ed and James keep Connor busy and out of trouble. Connor respects both of them and loves doing guy stuff. They are his yin and yang on the male perspective of life.

We had arranged to meet at 8:00 at our usual spot under the 820 bridge that joins the towns of Lake Worth and White Settlement. It's a long, high bridge, and, even though we don't need the shade today, in the summer, it's the best parking and shove-off point. As we round the northwest curve of the freeway approaching Heron Drive, we see flashing lights on the westbound side of the bridge.

"Hmmm... I wonder what's going on." Jackie's antenna goes up. She plucks a scrunchie from her purse and ties her hair back, a habit I'm sure she's picked up from working scenes with me.

I drive on eastward to exit Cahoba Drive and turn westbound on the access road. James's big red truck and boat are pulled over to the edge of the road as we come close to the lake. He and Ed are standing on their toes in the bed of the truck in an attempt to see. We pull up beside them, Jackie and Connor rolling down their windows.

"Hey!" Connor hollers over the sound of the police helicopter circling above. "What's going on?"

James steps down from the tailgate. "There's a body floating in the water just over there where that boat is." He points at a boat under the bridge. "Looks like a woman in a red jacket with long hair."

Ed joins him and pushes his way to Jackie's window. He looks at me past Jackie. I can see from his expression that her presence has not escaped him, and I notice Jackie has released the long dark curls from the scrunchie.

"And... you are?" he says, holding out his hand.

"Jaa—" Jackie starts to say.

I interrupt. "Connor get out! Stay here with them. We'll go see what's happening." I turn to the back seat, pushing his gear at him.

Fishing pole in hand, he struggles to gather his belongings. "God, Mom, I'm going! Wait! I gotta get my box." James helps him and throws Connor's coat over his shoulder while Ed continues to leer at Jackie. She smiles back at him.

"We'll wait right here," Ed says, backing up as I put the car in gear and cut back into the road. We head for the pack of squad cars and men standing around. "You could've at least let me introduce myself!" Jackie blurts out.

"He's my brother! You'll have time for that later." I'm amused at the thought of them as a couple. Ed hasn't had much luck with women. He married Candy when he was twenty. She was a titty dancer, and he thought he could save her from a life of sleaze. He wanted to have children and live happily ever after. The fairy tale didn't end happily for either one of them. She went back to dancing while they were still married. One day, she ran off with a rich, older gentleman customer, leaving Ed heartbroken.

When the old man discovered she was pregnant, he dumped her. Several years later, in an attempt to get Ed back, Candy told him the little girl was his. He was so proud at the thought of being a parent. At my urging, he paid for parental DNA testing recently made available to the general public. He was disappointed to learn she was not his child. The whole thing left him scarred and skittish. Now he's just a big flirt behind a thick wall.

When we reach the police cars, Jackie shows her badge to the officer assigned. He writes down our names and affiliations, then lets us drive through. I can see Hap, head and shoulders above everyone else on the dock. He's using his hands to describe something. He is angry.

As the boat makes its way to the dock, we see the woman's body on the floor between two seats. Clad in blue jeans and tan boots, a dingy white rope is tied above one boot with the denim fabric pushed up exposing pale flesh under the knot. The opposite end is frayed and tied to nothing. The red quilted jacket is waterlogged and looks heavy. Her forehead is caved in a disturbing contrast to the bloated face with empty sockets. A large gaping wound just below the hairline pools water.

We get closer, and I hear Hap's angry words. "I'm telling you, that's her." Detective Hernandez grasps at Hap's arm in an effort to calm him. "That's April! That's the son of a bitch's third wife." He puts his hands up and rubs his face. "I was trying to get some protection for her. She lives out in Parker County and I wasn't gettin' much cooperation from them. Now, he's killed her too." He pushes his grey hair straight back.

His rugged handsomeness radiates through his frustration. He turns to see Jackie and me standing before him. "Thank God! You're alright!" He expresses confusion with a wrinkled brow. "What are you two doing here?"

"Just going fishing," I reply. "I would think this is kind of early for you. What are you doing here?"

It seems he's trying to justify with his explanation. "I left orders to be called immediately for any dead women in your age group. And there's a standing order for you not to be called."

"Oh! I didn't really expect that, but okay."

"Hap, nobody called us. We really did come to go fishing." Jackie points up the ramp. Connor waves from the bed of the truck. Hap waves back and forces a smile.

The body snatchers unzip a black vinyl bag and lay it out on the wooden planks. The handoff of the body is tricky from the wobbling boat to the steady dock. Her head flops back and the long blond hair whisks across the weathered boards of the pier. Strands of hair snag on splinters and let loose from follicles of decomposing flesh.

"Do you recognize her?" Hap asks me.

"I don't think so, should I?" I pretend I hadn't seen her a few days ago or overheard his earlier comments.

"It's April, Megan."

I turn in the direction of my car. I can't listen to this. "I can't do this Hap! I've gotta go." My feet can't find traction in the loose gravel and I slip.

He comes after me with Jackie close on his heels. Grabbing my arm, he catches my arm and spins me to face him, shouting.

"Megan, you don't have a choice! This is happening! You told me to find this bastard, and that's what I'm trying to do, but you've got to start helping me!"

My arm throbs in the grip of his large hand. "What do you want, Hap? What do you think I can do or say to help you?" I wiggle my arm free and try not to cry. Everyone's looking in our direction. Jackie's big round eyes sympathize but are unable to help.

"Go get James," I order her, pointing in the direction of the truck. Jackie finds traction and takes off running.

Hap glares at the crowd paused behind him. Everyone ducks, returning to their duties. They load the body in the white van, and it slowly drives away.

Detective Hernandez addresses Hap rather formally. "Lieutenant, it appears she was hit in the head. Looks like he didn't want this one found... tried to weigh her down, but the rope... well, it didn't hold. I'm gonna head on over to the ME's office. I'll stay for the autopsy and see what they say." He catches his breath and humbly waits for Hap's response.

Hap keeps his eyes on mine. "Sure, you do that. Let me know what the doc says." The Detective's seriously receding hairline rises with his eyebrows.

"Uh, the tow truck's here to get that old pickup." He points, hoping to gain Hap's attention. "Lieutenant?"

"Yeeesss." Hap breaks eye contact with me, turning to Hernandez. "It's registered to an April Elaine Cox. We're sending someone to the address now. Where should I have them take it?"

It's *the* blue truck, the one that's been following me.

"Secure it in the sally port back at the station." The detective nods and takes off.

"And Hernandez, don't let anyone touch it!" he shouts, grasping my wrist before I escape his reach.

James puts an arm around me. I sense he thinks I need protection from Hap. Although they've never met, they've each heard me talk of the other many times. I'm sure they sense a familiarity. James and I are very close, and I had shared almost everything about Hap, including my feelings for him.

"Hey, James, I've heard a lot about you. Hap, Henry Parks." Hap holds out a hand, and James shakes it.

Upon hearing the cop's name, James takes his left hand from my shoulder and puts it on top of Hap's in a double shake. "Heard a lot about you too—old man! James Brooks." James' brawny face displays a broad smile.

I look at Jackie, worried about Connor. "He's fine. He's with Ed at the truck and anxious to fish. Do you think we can get on with it?" She raises her hand against the bright morning sun and looks at Hap.

"Yeah, sorry to keep y'all from your fishing," he tells James. "But you'll have to go on down to the point or over to the marina to put in. We'll be searching this area for at least a couple of hours."

Jackie turns and starts walking back to the truck. "I'll let them know." She seems a little anxious to get back there herself.

"You know we could just head on over to the old cabin and put in there," James says, pointing directly across the water. I shoot him a look but it's too late—the words were already out.

"Your family has a cabin on the lake?" Hap asks James.

"Well, it's not our family anymore. It was Kurt's dad's place. I don't know if it's still in their family. It's deserted. The weeds have taken over the old place, but it used to have a nice dock and boathouse. You can tell from here the boathouse is on its way down." He points again. In the far distance, a structure juts up from the water, listing to one side. Hap strains to make out the spot.

"It's over off of Heron on Indian Cove. I drive by the place from time to time. We used to have some good times there, didn't we, Megan?" He jabs me with an elbow and slowly realizes my disapproving demeanor. "You alright, Sis?" James frowns and bumps my hip with his, knocking me off balance.

"Megan, can I have a few words with you?" Hap leans into my field of view. I turn to look at James. "You don't mind do you, James? I won't keep her long."

James glances at me. "Sure you're okay?" I nod, and he walks toward the truck.

"Well, well, isn't this interesting!" Keeping his voice low, he circles me. "Is this something you just didn't think was important? Or did it just slip your mind?"

My feet firmly planted, I cross both arms under my breasts and stare at him. He pulls one hand free and marches me up to the others like a brat on her way to a good spanking. Connor watches us from the back of the truck, which was cleared through the barrier tape and now parked alongside my car.

"Mom?" Connor calls out. "You okay?" He reaches for me.

"She's fine Connor, just a little hard-headed. Jackie, she's to stay with you all day. No exceptions." Hap looks straight into my eyes and through clenched teeth asks, "Got it?"

I sigh. "Okay! I got it."

I suspect Hap refrains from shouting, not wanting to excite Connor. "I'm gonna get this guy, and I don't wanna be worried about you." He leans into my ear. "You're the last one, Megan. The only one left." He straightens his overcoat lapels, and we watch him get in his car. He's on the radio before the door closes. Gravel flies. If Kurt is at the cabin, it will only be a matter of hours until he is in custody. Of this, I have no doubt.

17

*E*arly the following morning, with the weather holding, I talk Jackie into a run. We drive the distance to my old alma mater, Eastern Hills High School. The clouds roll in as sunbeams shine through the chunky grayness, with a stray finding a sacred spot to illuminate. We park close to the less-than-perfectly manicured track. In the years since I'd spent many hours on these fields, the Fort Worth ISD has suffered financial setbacks. The once pristine campuses cry out for attention. I need familiarity, the comfort of a routine to escape the harsh realities.

"You wouldn't know it to look at now, but this used to be a beautiful area. There were green lawns that went on past the elementary school up there on the hill."

Jackie turns to see as I motion to the east. "Sad, it could be renamed Cement Hills now. What happened?" Jackie asks.

"The owner of a cement company and a Fort Worth ISD administrator learned if they kept the bids under a certain amount, few people would ask questions about improvements to school properties. So they cemented every patch of grass owned by Fort Worth ISD, save the football fields. They made a lot of money off the taxpayers."

We begin a slow jog, in step.

"Weren't they indicted a couple of years ago?"

"Yeah, and they were both found guilty." I glance skyward and pick up my pace, leaving her behind. "We better hurry. It's gonna rain."

A slow drizzle begins. The rising sun was warming the air. Now the clouds block it and a chill settles in. I find the beat in the fast-paced guitar strumming from my radio headphones and land my right foot in time to it. My mind replays the events of yesterday and seeing Kurt and April at the stock show on Monday. We haven't heard from Hap. I wonder if he's found Kurt, and if I should've told him that I saw the two of them together. He just seemed so angry. I knew he'd be more upset with me for not telling him when I saw him that day in the live-stock barn.

The vision of April being lifted from the boat won't leave my head. I've never worked any water death scenes, but from my training, it looks as though, with the eyes missing and 'washer woman' hands, she could have been in the water a few days. Her red, puffy jacket stretched tight across her swollen body.

Was she killed on Monday, the day I saw them together? Poor April, she wasn't very bright. It seems her emotional challenges made for a hard life, but she didn't deserve that. Was she just begging for someone to love her? Even from the man who took advantage of her and deserted her child as well? How did she end up in the lake?

The water beads on my skin, and with each rhythmic swish of my hands, I throw off droplets. I don't see Jackie on the track anymore. My emotions unleash, I let the tears flow to wash out the visons in my head. I finish eight laps. Moisture covers my face. I wipe my eyes and lick the salty diluted tears from my lips. As I walk to the far end of the field I can see a patrol car along-side of mine, driver's sides together. Jackie's sitting in the driver's seat of my car, and as I top the concrete hill, the patrol car pulls away. I shake my wet ponytail as I run to the car and, using my damp t-shirt as a makeshift towel, dry my face and arms.

She starts the car, grinding it into reverse. "They got him!" Shivering, I pull the seat belt across my shoulder.

18

WEDNESDAY, FEBRUARY 23, 1995

The stale, mildewed odor of the Tarrant County Jail fills my nostrils, and the noise of cranky babies disturbs me as I wait in a long line. Wives and girlfriends attend to the spawn of the incarcerated they've brought for viewing. Impatient with the pace of shuffling visitors, I shift my weight from one hip to the other. Signs taped on the window of the guard's booth warn:

NO BEEPERS OR PURSES BEYOND THIS POINT
DRESS CODE: NO SHORTS, NO SKIRTS OR DRESSES ABOVE
THE KNEE, NO SLEEVELESS SHIRTS

AND ADDED in bold capitals below:

NO SPANDEX

ARMS CROSSED, I shift my weight again, hoping no one will notice my sweater barely touches the top of my jeans. Though not specifically mentioned, I fear if my attire is judged inappropriate, I'll be told to leave and this day, along with the time I'd spent deciding exactly what to wear, wasted. The slightest lift of my arms reveals my tan flat stomach. I want him to want me as he feels the sting my words inject. Kurt'll wish he'd been nicer to me or left me alone altogether.

"Ouch!" The brat in the arms of the woman behind me grabs a handful of hair, snapping me from my recurrent vengeful daydream. I should turn around and tell her, *Run, get as far away as you can from the son of a bitch you're here to see. I don't know him, but I know you'll never be able to trust him. Go! Make a life for yourself without him!* She wouldn't heed my advice. I didn't listen when Kurt's own father tried to warn me.

Finally, we're herded like cattle through the procession of forms and metal detectors. My cynical state of mind doesn't mask my bewilderment in this unfamiliar world. A female deputy hands me a black card. I inspect it, a big white eleven on one side with a small white three and yellow S on the other.

In sharp Texanese, she asks, "You never been here?" *Here* is raised an octave above the previous words in disbelief. As a crime scene investigator, I've helped put a lot of people here, but I'd never had a reason to visit any of them before today.

I shook my head. "No."

The navy uniform is an insult to the Rubenesque woman. Curds of cellulite ripple beneath the stretchy polyester suit that should've been replaced two sizes ago. She snatches the card from my hand. "Okay, honey, go through the doors and then to the right." A long orange fingernail points behind me. "Right there, see? There are three elevators. Just stand in front of one of them. It will open. When you go in, hold this side up to the camera in the elevator." She flashes the eleven at me. "When the door opens, look at the map on the wall, find S," she says, tapping the S with a two-tone fingernail. "Then when you're done visitin', show this side here with the three to the camera and it'll bring you back down here. Got it?"

I nod my head. "Thank you." I walk over to the row of elevators. One opens, and I get in. George Orwell's *1984* comes to mind. This feels like a science fiction movie. The elevator is stainless steel, no buttons, no choices. *What if I change my mind? Who is watching me from the camera behind the black glass?* Before my panic rises to uncontrollable proportions, the door opens to uninviting concrete floors and walls. There's the map on the wall. Now I panic.

My fingers and toes are freezing as my underarms sweat. Nervous shaking begins as I pace in front of the elevators trying to regain my composure and brace myself for the task ahead. An elevator door opens with a sudden jolt, in unison with the shock to my entire body. A round Hispanic woman emerges, directing her little chicks. Never looking at the map, she appears all too familiar with the routine. They scurry around me and disappear.

I examine the diagram. If I go left, the S cubicle will be on my right. The partitions are stenciled with the appropriate letters on soundproof steel mesh. Metal stools are bolted to the floor of each stall. I locate the S stall. Through thick glass and a couple of pink lipstick prints I see an almost identical empty stall. Names and initials enclosed in hearts are scratched along the pale green borders of the windowsill and the shallow shelf below. A telephone receiver hangs on the wall to my right.

I can leave. *Am I ready for this?* I've rehearsed it so many times, how could I not be?

With damp palms resting on the cold metal shelf, I hang my head and watch my hair dance and tickle the back of my hands. A moment of whimsy before the expected gloom descends. Muffled sounds from the empty stall in front of me tell me I'm committed. I lower my butt to the stool and open my eyes to meet his.

His grey-green eyes are as cold and unpleasant as the walls surrounding him. I never met a man more handsome. Perhaps because I never loved a man as much as I loved this one. Aching in my heart does little to slow its rhythm.

The square jaw and flared nostrils reflect his aggressive nature. Suppressed fury writhes and my stomach burns. The lack of devotion must be prevalent in my eyes because he reaches for the handset first. His broad shoulders are constricted by the khaki jail attire resembling scrubs. A plastic ID band similar to a hospital bracelet circles his wrist. Slightly graying hair at the temples matches the premature gray streak at his hairline. The terror of this place is etched on his face and he exudes an aura of desperation. I relish in the justice of it.

Why does God dish out the best looks to those who deserve them the least and inflict the most pain?

He mouths *I love you.* I stare at him with disbelief. When he realizes I'm not going to echo it back, his expression of terror becomes wounded. I pick up the receiver and hold it to my ear.

"I've missed you." He puts his palm on the glass and wiggles his fingertips. Ever the salesperson, his enticing words are meant to sway me.

I don't know why, but my rehearsed words seem irrelevant now. He's doing all the talking and with six years of reflection, it's clear to me he never gave me a straight answer. He could always talk a blue streak with no prompting, but there were never any explanations. His answers only made more questions.

I let him ramble on, tuning him out. Something about, "I haven't seen Kacy for years," and "I swear, Megan, I didn't kill anybody! I was with you, remember?" He taps the glass to get my attention. "Megan? You've got to tell them I was with you!" His panicked shouts draw the attention of a guard, and he warns Kurt to quiet down.

Suddenly, I know why I'm speechless. It's the hurt in his eyes and the pain of betrayal I'm seemingly able to inflict without a word. It feels good.

He switches to a feeble tactic of pleading helplessly. The best sales pitch of his life, praising me as his sole savior. I return my attention to the cube. Through blubbering tears, he mouths, *I'm sorry*. Finally, he's sorry. I pick up the receiver.

He whispers, "There's money Megan, you just have to go get it. Please, will you do that?" He wipes his nose on a sleeve.

"Excuse me, what did you say?" Money? He has money?

"I said there's money, but obviously I can't get to it. Nobody knows about it. I need you to go get it for me. I'll split it with you, if that's what you want."

His statements tumble in my head. I pull the *I have money* one out first. "Where did you get it?"

"I can't go into all that now. Will you do it? If you'll get me outta here, we'll be set, Megan."

"Something tells me, if you weren't sitting over there with me out here, you would've never told me about any money. Am I right, Kurt?" All I want is confirmation that he'd screw me over again if I wasn't his only means of escape from this hell.

"No, of course not, Megan, that's why I came back. I was waitin' for the statute to run out. Then I'd come back for you and we'd go get it—the money. I... well I had two keys to a storage box. Let me back up. You remember when we went to London?"

"Yeah, I remember." Doubting every word he says, I let him continue.

"Well, before I closed the business in Louisiana, I stashed the funds in a bank account on the Isle of Man in the name of Alex Ward. Then when we went to England—remember when we went up to the Cotswolds and we stayed in that little old lady's house, the bed and breakfast?"

"In Cirencester? Where you dumped me?"

"I didn't dump you. I flew over to Castletown, got the money out of a bank there and put it in a locker at the Mount Murray Golf Club. I paid it up for ten years." He speaks softly, just above a murmur.

"How much? Hold on! You already had a new identity? You were planning to leave me way back then?" I want to break through the glass barrier between us and strangle him.

"It was just insurance, Megan, that's all!"

Tired of holding the receiver, I switch hands quickly, not wanting to miss a word of his decisive plan.

"How much money, Kurt?" On the verge of tears, I'm reminded of the uneasy feeling I had and his suspicious behavior on that trip.

"A lot."

"How much, Kurt?"

Lowering his voice to barely audible, he tells me. "It was close to a million."

"Dollars?" I shriek.

"Shh, will ya. Yes, it was dollars. Now it's about half that in pounds. There's a key behind the G. Harvey. It's still there over the TV, right? You said you still have it."

"*Turning the Lead*? Sure, it's still there, but there's no key," I lie. "I've moved it since then. Don't you think I would've noticed?"

At one time, a menagerie of Texas artists' oil well–themed prints decorated his office walls. But the prize of his collection was *Turning the Lead,* depicting a stormy cattle drive. He boasted, "Even in the most unlikely scenario, it epitomizes my ability to steer investors right to their checkbooks."

I actually found the key months ago, but I had no idea what it was for. It fell into the mass of cables and dust behind the TV.

"The key is there. I wrapped it in paper and put it under the certificate. Look, you'll see. Megan?" Kurt taps the phone on the glass. "Megan?"

In slow monotone I speak. "You said two keys. Where's the other one?"

"No, I didn't." His eyes don't leave mine.

"Yes, you did."

His gaze lowers to witness his thumbnail chip loose paint. "I lost it."

Now I know his motive. He wanted to get to the key and

abandon me again without anyone realizing he'd come back at all.

"So the real insurance is the key you left in the G. Harvey? You wouldn't have come back at all if you hadn't lost the other one." Feeling somewhat vindicated by his silence, I go on. "You deserted me. You left me broke and alone to put together a life from the little pieces you left behind. Did you ever think about me? Did you ever wonder if I'd survive or care if I didn't? Did you think about the boys? Mine and yours—you abandoned them too," I whisper. "We didn't deserve that. And now I find out you planned do it all over again. You know, Kurt, an idea came to me that first day at the lake. As a matter of fact, you said it. You gave me the idea yourself. Do you remember what you said? What you used to say all the time?"

His eyebrows come together.

I quoted him. "They'd be better off dead."

Does he understand what I've done, or will it dawn on him when he realizes the million-dollar gift he's just given me?

He's the only witness to a subtle confession, and his word against mine is worthless. Now he'll pay the ultimate price for what he did to me with the one thing he values most... his freedom.

19

8 MONTHS AGO, FRIDAY, JULY 2, 1994

*T*he grocery store appears as a time-lapsed film of ants attacking a food source. A common scene on the Fourth of July weekend, with cookouts, picnics, and family get-togethers. People in the parking lot are clad in shorts and sandals, attire to beat the stifling humidity. The high temperature is debilitating to some, but not me. It's invigorating, especially after coming out of the frosty, air-conditioned store. The heat from the blacktop rises to warm my legs.

A peaceful weekend of solitude awaits me. I've just bought a month of groceries for myself and two teenage boys. Grocery shopping is a chore I detest. I *could* get one of the boys to do it for us, but I don't think we'd survive a month on the "Three Ds"—Doritos, donuts and Dr Pepper. As they say, it's their balanced diet. I'm sure they'll throw beer in there someday, and I'll remind them it doesn't start with a D.

If I hurry, I'll catch Ian and Connor before they're off to their dad's. Then they can lug these heavy paper sacks from the trunk. A long weekend alone to rejuvenate is my plan. With Ian's graduation, family and friends flew in from all over the place, and some lingered on to be Cowtown tourists. I've seen more of Fort

Worth in the past four weeks than in the past ten years. Ian and Connor always spend the Fourth with their father and step-mother, Callie. Glynn is the proverbial party animal and the boys love the helter-skelter atmosphere at his house, on occasion. Callie keeps them in line. She loves my boys as much as I do. The Irish girl I wanted to be, with the red hair and the cute flirty freckles, she's genuine. I can't figure out what she sees in Glynn, though.

My mind is a whirl of thoughts as I arrange the piles of food in the trunk. There's the shopping I still need to do for Ian's dorm room. The uncertainty of what he will need his first year away on a college campus is too stressful for me to contemplate. With one fluid motion, my mind hours ahead of itself, I close the trunk lid, open the car door, and slide behind the wheel. I push the key into the ignition, and my movements slow when I see it. The symbol of love stares at me. I thank God there is no one here to witness my reaction. Wedged under the wiper blade is a playing card... the two of hearts.

Time becomes liquid and I'm rushed backward, to a cool rainy day. We lay on the sofa, the magnetic warmth of our bodies bonding us. Arms and legs entangled, an embrace that drew us into each other, making us one. I remember a time long ago, not of this life but another, when I was different and *he* was different. I recognize the soul, not the person. Kurt recruited me into studying metaphysics, and this became our only way to experi-ence transcending our bodies and traveling beyond this physical plane together. He claimed he'd experienced it many times. His tales of something so taboo enticed me to play with my spiritual world.

Studying the metaphysical realm began a journey that reshaped my attitudes and beliefs. Not only my beliefs on the afterlife, but my outlook on the here and now. My spirituality was adjusted and reconfigured to include dimensions I think non-scientists can't fathom.

The vision places me on a deserted dirt road. Danger hangs heavy in the air. Someone wants us dead, and my beloved is injured. I sense, because of a betrayal... my betrayal. I hold a scarf to his ribs in a futile effort to stop the bleeding. My heart pounds as I brush the hair back from my cheek and feel grit on my face. If only I had understood the consequences of my words, of my thought, maybe I would have understood the depth of the situation.

He is blond with a strong muscular build. Even though I know he is dying, he insists I get us to a safer place where we won't be seen. The urgency in his voice frightens me. Long red curls hang past my hands and get in the way as I nurse his wounds. My corset is tight and makes it hard to breathe. He tells me goodbye and utters words of love. "Please don't forget me, I will always love you. Our love will surpass time." His breathing grows rapid, then slows.

What happened? What have I done? There's nothing I can do now to prevent his death, and I realize the wrong I have committed. My love, my one true love, believes I betrayed him. He is dying, and there's nothing I can say to change it. I'm scared! They're coming for us, and I don't understand why. I can't remember. It's so far in my past, I can't bring it forward, no matter how hard I try. I lie entangled in his arms wondering what I did and why. How must I pay for this atrocity I served upon him?

Kurt tells me of a memory he's having at the same time. His words clarify the vision I see. I wonder how he sees what I'm seeing. He says he is injured, a wound in his side is making it difficult for him to breath—we must hide, they are coming for us. "Who?" I ask. He doesn't know, but we must move out of their view.

"They must not find us or we will die! Don't you understand? They will kill us!" Kurt jerks his arms wildly. He's not himself as we lie on the sofa.

Angry words spew. "How could you have done this to me?"

"What? What did I do?" I don't understand what happened, as I slip between consciousness and sub-consciousness. It wasn't a dream—I wasn't asleep. How did Kurt know what I was seeing and feeling? I never spoke aloud. Or maybe I did and don't remember. I attribute it now to us being in such a relaxed state of mind, it was a shared, past-life memory. As time goes on, though, I wonder...

I've told very few people, only ones I felt would be receptive to this kind of experience. They nod their heads and say, "How interesting." Or, "You know, I believe anything's possible."

How can two people be so spiritually connected and one betray the other so easily? How could I have betrayed him in another life so long ago that I don't even remember it now? And how could he betray me and our love in this life so easily. Was he paying me back on some cosmic level? Was I repaying a karmic debt that on a conscious level I couldn't possibly understand, or was it all another scheme? Is he such a trickster, a master of deception?

I'm thrust to a more recent point in time. He left on May 6th, a Friday night. I remember the date because of the first national telecast of a Garth Brooks concert from Texas Stadium. We had planned to watch it. We never did. I know he loved me. He wasn't obsessed with me. He was possessive, but not to the point of controlling like I'd known with Glynn. He just loved me. The night he left, he brushed my cheek with the back of his hand with tears in his eyes. He slid his hand down my outstretched arm, gripping my fingertips as he backed away. "Please don't forget me. Remember I love you. I will always love you."

Then, he was gone. I found comfort in his closet, full of his shirts and suits. I grabbed handfuls, buried my face, breathed him in, and cried. I just sat and cried, wondering where he was. I hid my grief in the closet, hoping the boys didn't know how much I hurt.

Does he still love me?

Five weeks later, I realized I was pregnant. It wasn't just the stress of my life being turned upside-down that caused me to miss a period. The memory of those days became a blur, an unreal time of just putting one foot in front of the other. Alone to pay the IRS and survive the mess he left in his wake. I struggled to get an education and raise two kids broke. I told no one. I called a women's clinic and made an appointment for a Friday. It was tough scrounging together enough money. I called in sick and went to the clinic, all alone. I was so ashamed at what I was about to do that I couldn't hold my head high enough to see three feet in front of me. Even though I'd gone to an area of town where I knew no one, I still feared someone would recognize me, someone would know. God would tell my grandmother.

The woman behind the counter handed me a clipboard with papers to fill out and a pen.

"Honey, do you have someone here with you?" the woman asked looking behind me as if my companion were hidden.

I looked up. "No, ma'am."

"Well," she kind of chuckled. "You're not going to be able to drive after this." She took the clipboard from my hand.

"I don't live very far; really I think I'll be okay." That's when I noticed all the girls with their boyfriends in the room. I wondered with whom I could possibly share this burden.

"You could go ahead and finish the paperwork today and we'll make another appointment for you, but we can't accept the liability of letting you leave here on your own." I pushed the clipboard back at her, feeling more alone than ever, and left, my mind a total void.

At that point in, I felt rejected and deserted by every man in my life. This was more proof that it would never change. If I was going to make it in this life, I had to change. I vowed to make it alone. This experience was no exception. Some women seemed to have their daddy or some man to rescue them. Not me. Where was my savior? My dad left me. I knew who he was and where he was, but he never seemed to be there when life got too tough to handle. Today wasn't any different. There was no one to hold my hand and walk me through the steps to carry this out; to help me justify my actions. He wasn't there. Whoever he was, he wasn't here. My anger grew. Kurt was forcing a decision on me I should've never had to make.

I swallowed my pride and called Ed, my younger brother. He couldn't save me, but he knew the hell I'd been through in the last few weeks. When Ed's broken heart needed rational healing, he'd come to me for my no-nonsense advice. If anyone could understand my sanity level and the desire not to bring a child into the mess my world had become, it was him. We drove to the clinic without a word and sat in the waiting room hand in hand, an internal stark contrast to the "real" couples there.

The nurse called my name, and Ed gave me a hug. "Do what you gotta do, Sis." He hugged me again real tight and kissed my cheek. I followed the nurse. I turned to look back, so grateful for a non-judgmental brother and friend. Ed desperately wanted children of his own and even though this wasn't his child, I felt I betrayed his dream.

In a sterile room, the nurse told me to disrobe, and I did so. She systematically placed goo on the end of a wand, pressed it around on my abdomen for the sonogram, and left the room with a concerned expression. She returned with the doctor.

"Megan," his mature voice was low and disconnected. "It appears to be twins." He looked at the printout, not at me.

A thought flashed through my mind of me running out to Ed, unable to continue, with the revelation of twins.

The doctor paused. I assumed he was waiting for me to gasp or wail. I did not. "Do you want to continue?"

If I don't want one, why in the world would you think I want two? Or are you just trying to make me feel twice as bad?

"Yes." I laid back and closed my eyes as tears slowly flowed down into my ears.

Internal numbness insulated my conscious world. The whole

ordeal was painful from beginning to end. They ripped life out of me, and part of my soul went with it. The little blue tablets they gave me didn't help much. My body felt as though I had experienced pregnancy and childbirth in a few short weeks. My hormones ran rampant. I didn't know what abortion really was. Biology classes gave me an understanding of the process, but I wasn't prepared for the emotional part. It all changed that day. I would never be the same again, wounded and deserving of any horrific punishment God could bestow. And he did. I hated God and the religion of my birth for placing the weight of unforgivable sin on me.

Ed got me home and tucked into bed, telling the boys that I was very ill and needed plenty of rest. They checked on me and went on with life, schoolwork and chores, TV and video games. This was unlike anything Ed had ever witnessed. He got me through the part I couldn't do alone, and left after I assured him I was going to be okay.

I wasn't okay. The next day I awoke in a pool of blood, a lot of blood. I was scared. Not for my health, but that someone would find out what I had done. I couldn't go to my doctor. I would have to tell her about the abortion. Unable to keep up with the expensive premiums, I lost my insurance after my divorce from Glynn. Death seemed the only way out. I cleaned up the bloody mess at a slow pace, to avoid passing out. I got myself back to bed and didn't wake up for two days. Ed came to check on me, but finding me asleep, he didn't disturb me.

Ian and Connor had the run of the house for the whole weekend, so they weren't overly concerned. I didn't go to my classes that Monday, but I managed to get the boys off to school, leaving macabre instructions for Ian.

"Honey if you can't wake me when you get home from school today, you should call Ed. I've put his number here by the phone."

My pale, sickly appearance must have scared him. "I'll stay home with you. Maybe we should call the doctor or go to the hospital?" He handed me a glass of water from the bedside table. "What can I do, Mom? You look so sick."

"I'll be fine. Just check on me. Please come straight home from school today. I'm sure it's just the flu or something. I'll be fine." When he left, I fell asleep.

"Megan... wake up!" I heard Ed's voice. He patted my cheek and grabbed my arms, lifting me out of the bed, and shook me.

"Ian called me before he left for school." Ed took the boys to Glynn and stayed with me for two days. He brought me back from the death I sought to consume me. I wanted the physical ailment to claim my hollow body and let me escape the devastation my world had become. I would be fine, eventually. One day rolled into the next and life continued. I went back to classes and work and thought about Kurt every day. I looked at every driver of every vehicle on the road, knowing that one day I would see him. He'd realize his mistake and come home. Some days, I thought I did see him. I'd follow some innocent man until I could get a better look, only to discover it wasn't him. It would have been easier if he'd died and I'd buried him. Then I wouldn't look anymore. Life was different. I became different. I returned to the closet.

While paying off the IRS and the bankruptcy, I managed to pay the bills with student loans and child support. It was a challenge to stay in school, but I knew it was my key to eventual success and independence. I sacrificed time with the boys to work and study. They spent many nights fending for themselves because I was with a tutor or researching in the library. Time progressed. Ian excelled at basketball, and Connor struggled to get passing grades. I took an intern position at the crime lab, mostly washing dishes, making up reagents, and assisting on crime scenes. It was heaven to me. There weren't any women working crime scenes. I felt like a pioneer, the pioneer mascot of my university.

Shortly afterward, I graduated with a Bachelor of Science, double majors, Biology and Chemistry. A full-time chemist position opened in the lab, and Sam offered it to me. After all was official, I was drafted into the on-call investigator's position. The overtime hastened my ability to pay off the student loans I'd depended on during the lean years. I began to save money for Connor's education, but I was counting on the bulk of the costs of his tuition to come from his father. It was evident he wasn't going to get a scholarship like his brother.

Life was smooth. The boys fought like brothers do. Occasionally there was a household emergency repair, and that was our only drama.

Once I finished school, I had time to think. I wondered where Kurt was. I wondered who was with him and if he was happy. I romanticized his choice to leave. He was saving me from a life of consequences because of his poor behavior. Surely, he would return to me someday, the love of his life, right? I didn't hear from him. I thought of us at least once every day. I replayed it over and over again. One day I'd grieve and the next I'd be angry. I still couldn't make it make sense, and I'd force myself to stop thinking. I'd busy myself with one project or another. There were many ballgames to attend. I never missed one after I finished school. There was a lot of catching up to do. The boys enjoyed a return to family life with traditional hours.

At times, Ian or Connor started to recall a fond memory of Kurt, but quickly let it go. I guess they still saw the pain on my face. The boys enjoyed Kurt immensely. He was a real dad. Playing football in the yard, coaching little league, boating, fishing and skiing trips. Kurt was always spending time with them doing guy stuff. I know they missed him terribly. It's not just what he did to me, but my sons and his boys, too.

Ian unsuccessfully encouraged me to go out with his coach for a while. Now that my excuse of being too busy with school was over, he renewed his quest. I met the man several times at Ian's games and at teacher visitation night. He was a better-than-average-looking man, physically fit, tan and tall. I discovered he was now Connor's history teacher. The boys began double-teaming and wore me down. We dated a couple of times. He was intelligent and seemed genuinely attracted to me, but I never felt any electricity. Even though he claimed there was chemistry, I didn't feel it or the need to go on dating him. After that failed attempt, I didn't care to date anyone. I settled into a schedule of work and happy hours with Hap.

Every now and then, someone set me up with a friend. There were the aloof ones and the busy ones, desperately pretending to fit me into their busy schedules. The worst were the macho cops commanding such presence in uniform, but out of uniform, they became creepy. One even asked if he could call me "Mommy." Another had a closet-sized safe and bragged of owning more than a hundred guns. He scared me. After I got rid of him, he'd call and not say a word.

After a couple of dates and a go in bed, I was ready to get back to my effortless life. I hated them all for loving me, wanting me, expressing feelings I could never return. None were strong enough for me, to handle me, to fight a good fight without backing down. The only man I feel has strength and passion to match mine is Hap. He's safe, and if I don't get too close, he can't hurt me. He'll never leave me.

Deep within, I still ache for Kurt. How could he leave me so shattered? Mentally and physically scarred, not happily married, attending graduations, charity events, and college basketball games seated next to my husband. Like the mothers of my sons' friends. I never found a connection with anyone like I had with Kurt. Dating was expected of me, so I did it.

THE SILENT PLAYING card screams at me. The stifling July heat no longer comforts me. It only reminds me how cold and brittle I am, ready to break.

We used the two of hearts as a secret message to meet at his fathers' lake cabin. In the beginning of our relationship, we didn't want anyone to know we were seeing each other, so we met at the cabin on Lake Worth. It wasn't that we were doing anything wrong. Our boys grew up together, and we didn't want them to be disappointed if we decided not to continue the relationship. Before we were together as a couple, we spent many summer days there with our spouses and our boys. Kurt's boys spent most of their summer days with their grandfather on the lake, fishing and hanging out at the cabin. They helped their granddad take care of the property. After Kurt left, his dad was in a bad car accident that left him homebound, and the place began to decay. Kurt's sister moved to Dallas after college. Excessively overweight most of her life, she never cared for the bathing-suit life at the lake. Understandable.

My time there began the summer before Connor's birth. I was seventeen, in love with my life, chasing Ian and pregnant. Glynn didn't mind me spending time away from home when I was big and pregnant. In his mind, was there less chance of me "sleeping around" on him? I never did, but he always accused me. That summer, Kacy and I planned to spend a lot of time together. She'd show up, drop her boys off, and leave with a ruse of a short errand. Then she'd return hours later without a plausible explanation. She did sleep around. She knew I knew, but she never trusted me with the details. The cabin turned into her daycare.

As time passed, his father and sister seldom used the cabin, so when we began meeting there, we knew we wouldn't be discovered. Even after we married it was our escape from all the kids and ex-wives. Kurt was such a romantic; he planned the music, exquisite food, and our favorite scented candles to provide light.

I sit in the boiling July heat and stare at the playing card, unable to breathe. Suddenly becoming aware he's probably watching me, hoping to see my reaction. I start the engine, my left leg shakes uncontrollably as I hold in the clutch and shift into reverse. At that moment I don't know, truly know, what to do.

At home, I conquer the tasks at hand and send the boys off to Glynn and Callie's, with their annual Fourth of July warning of how great-aunt Maureen lost a hand in a firecracker accident as a child. It's an exaggerated tale of caution, passed down from my mom about an aunt we never met, but it's worked so far. At eighteen and fifteen, they roll their eyes and bounce away in Ian's new Jeep, his father's graduation present.

A sleepless night of indecision, I search the closet for the shoe box containing my letters written to Kurt after he vanished. Written when I was sad, angry, or lonely and scared, never thinking they'd get any closer to him than the box I kept them in. Tossing it on the bed next to the two of hearts, I gather my courage with the covers around me, reading them at random. I relive the weeks of heartache in a haphazard timeline, my heartrending words of pain in one letter turning into ferocious ranting anger and regret for the abortion with the next. The expressions of feeling so alone brought bouts of depression and contemplated suicide. Ian and Connor's images were the only thing between me and the depths of hell, into which I could have so easily thrown myself. Without Ed, I would have succeeded. Those babies would be five years old now, five. Two little girls? Two more boys? Maybe one of each? I'll never know. I'll never forgive him for taking so much from me.

Stop doing this Megan! Why are you dredging up these horrible feelings of abandonment and anger?

The bottle under my bed helps me fight the past, so I can face the future. I know the curiosity will eventually win. I might as well get it over and be done with it. My tender eyes burn, and with one last sip of the whiskey, so does my throat. The pillow feels cool against my cheek. Alpha's snores lull me to sleep.

Groggy, I pitch the covers back and the letters flutter as a plan comes into focus. The dogs do their morning dance, eager to go outside. My first cup of coffee helps crystallize today's agenda. I'll go see him one last time. Then, after I contact the fugitive squad and when he least expects, they'll swoop in and take him. He'll finally pay for what he's done.

It didn't quite happen that way. I never called the fugitive squad.

20

SATURDAY, JULY 3, 1994

The cabin looks just as I remembered, although a bit worse for wear and neglect. The once beautiful flower gardens are now full of weeds. Bulbous purple heads sit atop the sturdy stalks of the surviving thistle. The revered national flower of Scotland, a mere weed in Texas, stands wilting in the July heat. Pale green paint is faded and peeling from the structure. The roof supports dead tree limbs still strewn about from the spring storms. Humidity hangs as heavy as the fear I wear. As the rain begins, I shuffle through the overgrown vegetation on the path to the front porch and instinctively quicken my pace.

What lies behind the door to the old lake cabin is someone I haven't seen in more than six years. A person I once felt so in tune with that I hungered for his every touch, his next breath. We were inseparable, locked together with ties I didn't understand, or want to, if it meant dissolution. The sky opens, thunder cracks, and I run. The door swings open at my arrival, and I freeze. There he is, looking much as the last day I'd seen him. He is strikingly handsome, now forty-one, his graying temples lending an air of distinction.

He is so unlike the visions in my dreams; pale, sunken face, missing teeth, thin and weak. I worried so. I feared he had become a homeless transient, alone, suffering every day. He couldn't look further from it. Kurt is tan, muscular, and freshly shaven, looking as though he's just come from a month-long vacation in the Caribbean.

I hesitantly walk in, shaking the rain from my hair. The interior holds the same early-seventies furniture and burnt-orange shag carpeting that were so popular in the heyday of this place. I smell the faint fruity scent of a candle but it does little to mask the persistent damp, musty odor. I feel his hands on my shoulders. With effort he turns me in his direction, but I pull away. My heart is as stagnant as the air. The cabin never had air conditioning and, with no electricity, an old fan sits motionless on the floor. I take two steps forward and turn to face him, out of arms reach. His face is puzzled.

"Did you think I would be happy to see you?" I ask.

"I hoped you would be." A wounded animal, he walks to the kitchen and pours a glass of wine, motioning with the bottle to see if I want some. Richard Marx's latest hit drones from a boom box that sits on a space heater in the corner of the room. Dual grills, eras apart.

I nod, and he pours me a glass. We make our way to the back porch and sit in quiet awkwardness. The oversized rocking chairs creak from long forgotten weight. Gnat-littered cobwebs cling to the eaves. Kurt watches me intently; perhaps he anticipates a quick left hook any second. Gastric juices churn. Every motion made seems nervous and exaggerated. The tranquil scene of thick St. Augustine leading to the water's edge brings me no reassurance about being here. I lean my head back and, with a heavy breath, fear he'll interpret my silence for contentment. "I…"

Kurt gestures out at the trees. "I found th—oh, I'm sorry. Were you gonna say something?" He drops his arm and turns to look in my direction.

"No, go ahead." I didn't really know what to say anyway. I'd just wanted to break the tension.

"Are you sure?" I nod. "Well okay. I found the old hammock out in the boathouse." He points to an ancient woven hammock suspended between an oak and a cottonwood. "It needs repairing, something to fill my time here. Maybe I'll tackle the boathouse when I can get out and buy supplies."

The rain falls with a steady pace. Another loud clap of thunder makes me jump, and he places his hand on mine. I don't pull away. I feel so sad about what we've lost, love immeasurable within the limits of time and space. With my other hand on top of his, he squeezes and I feel whole again. I lay my head on our hands and close my eyes.

"Where've you been? I waited and waited for you." I raise my head and examine his expression, wishing time would reverse. "Every day I thought you'd come back, but you didn't. You left me so alone, to face the debt and the questions and the shame." Tears well and trickle down my face.

I speak with a shattered heart and ragged breath. "I tried to be so strong. I held on every day. The boys never knew how I ached for you." I think of, but never mention, the abortion. I clench the arms of the chair, gasping for air between sobs.

"They never knew I cried every night for months trying to get over you. Ian and Connor were the only reasons I had for living most days." I release my grip and wipe the tears from my face. "How—*why* did you do this to me?"

He stands and lifts me into a comforting hug. "I'm sorry, Baby. I'm so... so sorry." The large, tan arms envelop me. "But I couldn't go to jail, not for one day. I would die there." A freshly showered fragrance blocks the recall of his libidinous pheromones still imprinted on my brain.

I push away. "You didn't call or write. I didn't know if you were dead or alive. I wondered if it had just all been too much and you committed suicide or if one of your investors had you killed. Then it dawned on me, I finally understood. You didn't love me... at least not as much as I loved you!"

He interrupts me. "How can you say that?"

"Because *you* had a choice! You had the power to come back to me. Power I didn't possess. I couldn't come to you. I *would* have come to you. I would've risked everything for you, given up anything for you and me—*us*—anything!" My breaths come in gulps as my body wrenches and shakes with the pain from so long ago. I stride through the house to the sofa and pull the letters from my purse. My tears give way to anger.

"Where were you? Birthdays, our anniversary, holidays, they all came and went with nothing, not a word!" I yell at him and shiver uncontrollably.

"I was here." He comes close as his voice trails off. "I was around, watching. I called many times just to hear your voice." He reaches out to me. "Just because you didn't see me or hear me doesn't mean I wasn't there. I couldn't let you see me. I know you could feel me watching you. The phone calls when no one spoke, that was me. Do you know how hard it was not to speak to you? Not to approach you, to touch you and tell you I love you?" He turns it all around. He's always been good at that. It was all about him, once again... all about him. He won. He's regained all the power he held over me.

"You did not!" I jerk my arm away from his grasp and throw the letters at his feet. "Here's my love, my anger, my life after you left!"

"Baby, I had to wait until enough time had passed. I couldn't be locked up. You remember how it was. You remember how Kacy and Missy made life hell for me. For us!" He steps on the letters and advances in my direction. "Do you think it would've ever stopped?"

I watch his weight crush the last bit of life from what I felt for him, boiling inside, but frozen in place. Suddenly aware of his disregard and realizing how hurt I am, he bends down to retrieve the letters and bundles them in his hands. "Like this! They did this to us!" The folded papers make a flapping noise as he shakes them angrily. "They'd be better off dead! Hell, they'd all be better off dead!" He returns my feelings to the floor and stomps away. Opening the screen door, he walks through and lets it slam.

On hands and knees, I gather the letters in a neat pile. He raves loudly as he paces on the back porch, waving a cigarette through blown smoke. The voice on the radio laments *I do love you... still.* Melancholy engulfs my heart. Holding the envelopes, I bow my head and clutch so many of our dreams that were swept away with his decision to abandon me.

"And the whole oil thing, I didn't take anything from the rich that they couldn't afford to lose. They invested and they lost. It's a gamble. I told them that when I took their money." He acts like he's the victim in this self-imposed tragedy. "I lost too! It wasn't like I kept *all* their money." He returns with a slam and pours himself another glass of wine, not offering me more.

Stuffing the letters back in my purse, I can't believe his callousness. "It doesn't matter to you that they gave you their money in good faith and you weren't actually using it to make them richer? Instead, you threw their money down empty holes and into your own pockets." I toss the purse to the sofa. "It's not about the women in your life, it's about your children—your boys, my boys. They love their father, and you left them. No explanations... no goodbyes."

"Those bitches would have continued to harass me for more and more child support. Don't get me wrong, I love my boys. I'm back now, and they'll get over it." He lays a hand on my shoulder. "You'll see, you'll get over it, too." I shrug his hand off me.

"You son of a bitch! Get over it? Are you crazy? Life went on, Kurt. Life went on without you. People have come and gone in our lives. Events you were never a part of occurred. Jessie died." Perhaps I detect a faint recollection of our Shitzu in his sorrowful frown.

"I'm sorry... I couldn't do it anymore! Not with the threat of prison on top of everything else." He rubs his head and paces. "Things had to happen, Megan, time had to pass. Surely you understand that. I knew if I waited long enough, the boys would be grown." Grabbing my shoulders, he gives a jerk then steps back suddenly, sensing my fear of him. "That Attorney for Mississippi has to let it go now that the statute of limitations will be up soon on the whole oil investment mess."

"Why did you come back, Kurt? You got away. No one knew where you were."

"Hell, Megan, I miss you. I miss my kids. I've been counting the days until I could be here with you. In a few months, Matthew will be old enough to come live with me—us—and no more paying *that* worthless bitch another dime."

My mind stumbles over numerous objections. Something's not adding up.

Us? No more child support? What about the six years you're behind? What if Matthew doesn't want to come live with you? Is there a statute of limitation on broken hearts and promises?

I stand in disbelief, paralyzed, convinced he's delusional. Awaiting my reaction, unsure what to say next, he continues to speak, but I hear none of it. The buffering fog lifts from me at that moment. I can't speak. I want to dispute his reasons for leaving and returning, but I remain silently appalled.

How can he so easily disregard my feelings, the horrendous mess he made of my life? I was a fool to mourn the loss of him.

A vision comes to mind of me, sitting in my closet clutching his shirts, breathing him in, crying profusely. My body twisted from the physical pain of loss and desperation. He's humiliating me all over again.

"You'll see, Megan. You still have the house, don't you?" If he's been watching me, he knows I still live there. "You finished school and you've got a good job, right? You did okay."

"Yeah, I graduated, no thanks to you. I had to sell everything of value to pay tuition. I guess you could say I'm doing okay now, but I wasn't in the beginning. The IRS put a lien on the house because of you, you bastard."

"You did what?"

"My engagement ring and your tools, I sold just about every-thing. Did you hear me? I almost lost the house, too. The IRS got your taxes out of *me*."

"The G. Harvey's? Please tell me you didn't sell my G. Har-vey's." His palms pressed together in mock prayer.

"Of course I did. They weren't worth as much as I thought they'd be, but they paid for a semester and books."

"No, no." Kurt turns his back to me and mumbles. "Those were mine. Where? Who did you sell them to?"

Is he laying claim to assets he abandoned?

"Yours? Are you fucking kidding me! Why are you so concerned about a few cowboy pictures?"

"Those were authentic, signed and numbered prints. Who has them?" He grabs my wrist.

"I sold them to a woman I worked with, her husband was a collector." I look in his eyes for a hint of their importance to him.

"So… you can buy them back?"

"They're gone, Kurt. He died last year and she moved to her sister's place in Alabama." Prying from his grip, I back away.

"I kept one. The one over the TV, the gold one with lightning, the cattle drive at the river. I forget what it's called. She already had one and it wasn't worth much anyway. I tried to find a buyer, but no one wanted it," I lie. I knew it was his favorite and worth much more than the others.

"*Turning the Lead*? You kept *Turning the Lead*? Yes." His shoul-ders relax and relief sweeps across his face.

After all he's put me through, turning my world upside-down, leaving a mass of destruction in his wake for me to clean up. Now he's bemoaning the loss of a few cowboy pictures. I shuffled through the mess and finally reorganized my life. Now he wants to come back and disrupt my neat little piles, bring embarrassment to me, to my family, all over again!

I've worn the shame of being his victim too long, maintaining a balance of love and hate all these years. An illuminated path of retribution lies before me.

I can kill him, but he wouldn't suffer long enough. He must endure the same mistrust and grief he put me through. Death is true freedom in his metaphysical realm of belief. Just in case it's true, I can't take a chance that death will reward him. His worst fear is prison. The ultimate payback is the misery captivity will bring. Other people's mistakes taught me well, and now it's time to put that knowledge to work.

He felt the women in his life had caused him to do the things he'd done, be the way he was. Now because of the women in his past, his life is going to change, all of it. His own will haunt him. *They'd be better off dead*. Let's see if he feels that way in a few months. He'll regret that statement.

"I'll have my life back, my boys back together again. We can pick up where we left off!" Excitement in his voice does little to persuade me.

I shake my head, separating thoughts of vengeance from a display of false compassion. *His life back?* The acidic bile of hatred is tough to swallow while brandishing the friendly face of a confidant. "I don't know, Kurt. Things are different now."

We embrace. I maintain a façade of defiant reluctance. With mock apologies, I concede not understanding the terrible life he endured while on the run all those years. He holds my face in his hands and brushes the dampness from my cheek. His familiar odor and kisses weaken my resistance and revive a passion I never believed I'd experience again. We find our way to the same squeaky bed where we spent so many hours, so many years ago.

He's as tender and attentive as I remember. I let the wine work for me and enjoy it for what it is… sex. Endless movement produces pouring sweat from our bodies, adding to the steaming humidity of the thunderstorm. I lick droplets from his chest, working my way down to his stomach and taking a mouthful of swelling flesh, bringing him to the brink. He never left me wanting more, and I always reciprocated. Never, before him, was I entirely satisfied, and not much after. Tonight is no exception.

My act is so good, so convincing. I just let go. "Oh, how I've missed your touch!" My body exudes sweat and regret.

He speaks all the words I long to hear, and in another time, believed. I mimic his responses, trying not to be cynical. I learned a lot about sex in the last six years, and I spare nothing from him. I make love to him with passionate vengeance while the anger burns inside of me. We reach simultaneous orgasm and I dig my fingernails into the meaty flesh of his buttocks wanting to leave a mark of the undeserving love he stole from me.

When we finish, he flings himself back on the wet sheets, "Holy shit!"

We fan ourselves. Wrapping me in his arms, he holds me close. I feel as though I'm going to suffocate and want to push away. I continue the pretense, brush the sweat from his brow and cup his jaw in my hand. I hover and kiss him softly. We talk about what has happened in our lives in the last six years.

"How did you hide for so long? Two private investigators couldn't find you." I sit cross-leg on the bed beside him.

"I changed my identity," he boasts.

"So, how'd you do that?" I ask, like I didn't remember our conversation many years ago.

"It wasn't that hard. I saw a grave, you know out in the old Stag Creek cemetery where my mother is buried in DeLeon?" His excitement raises the volume of his voice. I lift my glass of wine from the water-stained nightstand, take a sip and nod.

"I went to visit her grave after I left here." He visited her grave often when we were married. I thought perhaps he was apologizing for blaming her for the terrible abuses he suffered as a small child.

"I noticed the tombstone of a young boy, Alexander Clayton Ward, only three graves away from Mom's. He was born the year before me." He sits up motioning with his hands as he describes how he wrote down the boy's name, birth and death dates.

"I checked in the local phone book to make sure no one with that last name was living in town. 'Cause, ya know, I couldn't risk running into the kid's mother or dad at the courthouse. Then I went to the Comanche County Bureau of Vital Statistics and told them I had inherited some money, but I needed the death certificate to prove my only sibling was dead. It showed where he was born." He seems so proud of himself.

I smile and make believe I'm caught up in the execution of his plan. "He was born in Taylor County, August 18, 1956. So, I drove to Abilene with the death certificate and got the birth certificate. For the last almost seven years, I have been Alex Ward, from Abilene, Texas," he said with a twang of betrayal and his chest puffed out.

"I've lived all over since then. I went to San Diego and built houses, nice, big houses. Then I went up to Portland for a while. Before that, I sold my truck in LA. Ya know, I knew if I got stopped, the Texas license plates would come up as stolen sooner or later. I didn't really expect you'd keep making the payments."

He grabs the sheet, wraps himself and walks around the room like Cesar declaring a proclamation. "Well let me say, I *knew* you wouldn't be able to keep making the payments." So, he did give me a thought.

"Then I went to Mexico..." He goes on and on... something about the sandy beaches and not being able to find work... I try to appear interested. *Poor guy!*

Before I can ask about the women, we hear the distant pops of fireworks. He'll omit the women. I know there have to be a trail of them. Do they worry about him now like I worried about him then? How many of *them* did he leave brokenhearted and broke? The sheet trails behind him as he passes in front of me. I grab a corner and whip it away leaving him bare.

"Come on, let's go see!" I run out the screen door toward the lake with him close behind, snatching at the sheet. The streaming lights mirror in the water. He stands tall behind me and enfolds his arms into mine.

"I've dreamed of this moment every night since you left." I lie, a little.

"I know, Baby, me, too." He lies, a lot.

His cheek rests above my ear as we watch the colorful bursts in midair. "Stay the night, Baby."

"I can't. Connor and Ian will worry about me," I lie. They're at Glynn's and won't be home until late Sunday.

Over my protest to stay longer, he pushes my hair away and tenderly kisses the back of my neck, enticing me. We return to bed to lie on moist sheets. The sheer curtains sway slowly to the quick rhythm of the candle's flickering flame, and we outline a future together. Knowing the plan will never come to fruition, his embellishments of the details are moot, but I play along.

The persistent state of heightened anxiety for more than twenty-four hours has left me exhausted. We fall asleep in a loose spoon. His wrist drapes my waist.

Awakened by a noise, I lay still and ascertain my whereabouts. Kurt's arm is heavy and our contact flesh sweats. I haven't been asleep more than a few minutes. Snippets of the evening's conversations replay and further solidify my vow of revenge.

I could kill him now. Make him pay for what he's done. If I keep very quiet, I could get a knife from the kitchen and slit his throat while he sleeps. No one will ever know. His corpse will lay here and rot for months, maybe years. If anyone's missing him now, they don't know where he is. No one knows I'm here.

"What is it?" Kurt raises his head. "Did you hear something?"

"No." I jump up and scuttle around in the dark for my bra and panties. "I've got to go." His hand clutches my wrist and with a tug I fall to the bed. In a quick motion he places a knee on either side of me and secures both wrists above my head with one hand, sliding the other around my neck. For an instance I wonder if he suspects I'll reveal his hideout to the fugitive squad. I'm up to something, but he couldn't possibly know my intentions. Forcefully he presses his lips to mine... a painful kiss... a warning? With a flip of the wrist the bra sweeps past his cheek. I bow up and throw him off balance just enough for an escape.

"I said, I've gotta go!" I coerce a smile and hop from the bed.

Watching me intently, he doesn't bother to get up and help me find my clothes or walk me to the door for a proper goodbye. "Remember, not a word to anyone," he shouts when he hears the creak of the screen.

Yeah, not a word. I raise a middle finger at the wall and let the door slam behind me.

The dark, winding road follows the shore of the lake toward home.

Lightning bolts illuminate and booming thunder seems to hurry the cattle and vibrate the frame as I lift *Turning the Lead* from an upturned nail. The bright overhead light of the living room calls attention to the carpet's dire need of vacuuming. I place the large framed print on the sofa and inspect it. Nothing unusual on the front, I turn the glass to face the cushions and notice a slit in the paper backing just behind the envelope containing the certificate of authenticity. I tilt the artwork and carefully put a hand in to probe for, what?

What exactly am I looking for?

---

21

*T*here's nothing here. I stand back, arms crossed, and contemplate the brown paper. If there was something in there, it's gone now. Is it the envelope, maybe the certificate itself?

The depth of the old console television proves too great a distance, and the picture seems heavier with the weight of disappointment. I rest it on top of the VCR and step to the side, accidently knocking Connor's Atari game controllers to the floor. When I bend to retrieve them, I notice a small folded piece of paper trapped in the tangled wires and dust. Wedging myself in between the TV and a chair, I scoot the heavy set away from the wall. A rubber band encircles the bundle of paper three or four times making it easy to pinch between two fingers and pull to my palm. The rubber band is brittle and disintegrates as I pinch and pull it. I unfold the paper to discover a wide brass key. The fragile paper reveals a blue and green square with a black horse on it at the top of the page. I walk to the kitchen for better light. Under the square, the paper has deteriorated. At the fold, all I can read is Lloyds TSB. The printing on the page is very faint. I can make out some numbers and what appears to be a curvy large L with a line through it.

What the hell is this?

I place the paper in a magazine to flatten and preserve it for inspection under my microscope at work. The key is stashed in a pocket. Once the room is back in order, I retreat to the sanctuary of my bedroom, making a mental note to clean behind the TV.

Alpha circles his spot on the floor while Beta pushes the comforter into the required heap with her nose before curling up at the foot of the mattress. Flat on my belly, I stretch an arm under the head of the bed. Dust stirs a sneeze just as my fingernails dig into the engraving on the box, tipping it toward me close enough to grip. I carefully place another consolation prize in the box. Beta's concerned kisses remove my tears before I curl up under the covers.

IN THE DAYS THAT FOLLOW, a plan formulates. Kacy and Missy will be *his* victims. After all, they are the ones that made his life, our lives, most miserable. Poor feeble April never had the nerve to fight for herself or her child. I couldn't hurt April... I don't think anyone as dejected as her deserves to die.

Yes, Kacy first, then Missy, the source of his problems. If they'd left us alone, not been so demanding, maybe Kurt wouldn't have felt the need to deceive innocent people and steal from them. My own contempt for the two of them should make this easy enough. If I look hard enough, I may find actions not worthy of sustained life. But this isn't about them, this is about Kurt. Yes, I'll do it in order, Kacy first, then Missy, April spared. The decision to kill weighs my heart with the density of stone. I push aside sympathy for their loved ones and smother all feelings. Emotionless, I face each day entertaining thoughts of murder in order to recognize every opportunity to further my mission. Remembering episodes when Kacy and Missy infuriated me most helps feed my anger and hatred for them. I dwell on those times daily to provide stimulus for success.

Kacy was the absolute worst mother I'd ever met. While Kurt was at work during the day, she carried on an affair with a neighbor and would leave the boys home alone at a very young age. I caught her a few times, when we lived in the same apartment complex. Her compulsive lying hurt the boys many times after she and Kurt were divorced. His two oldest sons "unofficially" lived with us after Kurt and I were married. Many times, she'd promise to pick them up for the weekend or dinner and never show, never call, nothing, only to show up days later with an expensive toy or clothes, no doubt bought with the child support Kurt paid. Not that the punishment for lying is death, but breaking the hearts of those who love her is a crime she never paid for. *I* was the one who witnessed their repeated disappointments. *I* was the one who comforted them and made excuses for her. I didn't receive so much as a thank you from her.

Missy wasn't as cruel. She used Matthew as a pawn to win games of manipulation against Kurt for the sake of money. She wouldn't allow Matthew to spend time with his father if Kurt refused to pay for karate lessons or the newest athletic shoes Matthew demanded. She'd tell him if his father didn't buy him what he wanted, that meant he didn't love him. Matthew became a spoiled brat, throwing tantrums and spewing his mother's words when he came to visit. The house was peaceful without him.

I justify the price is worth the prize, Kurt's freedom. To successfully accomplish the task, I'll need to ensure the spouses are ruled out as suspects by forcing the lines of Kacy and Missy's deaths to converge at the origin—the ex of both. I spend hours daydreaming of the best methods. Blatant murder would require violence depicting rage. Staged accidents might be accepted as coincidence, whereas staged suicides using a gun appear easy, but close examination of blood spatter evidence could easily reveal the truth. Clean and quiet is the way to go, no action painted in blood and no attention garnered from noise. If it's meant to be, fate will deal me the right cards, and in a few weeks, I'll be able to put this all behind me. Just like the abortion, I'll block it out, resume my life and Kurt will live the rest of his life in hell. Two for two. After all, some might believe in the eyes of God, I've already murdered twice.

On a morning run, the first sign appeared—a long rope on the side of the road.

22

THURSDAY, AUGUST 12, 1994

*D*estiny delivers the necessary tools to me. Two weeks back, I received a case consisting of marijuana and several vials of fast-acting insulin. While identifying the vials, I came across valuable information. The PDR says it reacts within ten minutes and if a non-diabetic is given insulin, their body will react in much the same way as an insulin-dependent diabetic does if they don't take it. I know it won't be detected in an autopsy because our toxicology lab only checks for alcohol, medications, and street drugs. The biology section searches for diseases and biological abnormalities, such as enzymes of the heart after a heart attack. Neither looks for insulin unless the pathologist makes a specific request. And with today's technology, even if they did find it, they're unable to quantitate it.

Certain once I reseal the evidence, it will never be opened again, I bury a vial in my pocket. Most misdemeanor cases never make it to trial because the defendants usually agree to a plea bargain and the evidence is destroyed. If they inventory the items before destruction, they'll assume either the officer or the chemist miscounted. The insulin is only in the case for a couple of reasons—either the suspect thought he could sell it on the street or he's diabetic. In any case, he isn't getting it back, and a 50 milliliter vial is more than enough for both women.

I don't know if it'll be easy, but I do know, throughout my life, when faced with a difficult task, all I had to do was break it down into segments, systematically design a plan, and carry it through, one step at a time. Preparation and eliminating obstacles, both real and emotional, had cleared the paths, from dissecting a cat in anatomy lab to complex chemistry experiments, even abortion. This is no different, an unpleasant job that I must do well.

I've processed plenty of murder scenes and the evidence left behind. Now that I possess the bits and pieces to set this up convincingly, it's just a matter of establishing the opportune moment. Kacy's neighborhood is a new, very large subdivision. Her home is one of three completed and the only one occupied. There are model homes several blocks away. The neighborhood gives the appearance of seclusion, but it's actually located very close to a major freeway. During the day, the developing neighborhood streets buzz with construction workers. The cement trucks come and go like clockwork. It's a very different place after all the workers leave at dusk, quiet and still.

For two weeks, I watch and plan. Kacy's husband travels regularly, and she never has visitors. I arrive every day before dark and watch from a tree-lined hilltop a couple of blocks away. At dusk, with just a few lights on and undraped windows, it's like watching a fish swimming in a bowl. A couple of weeks into my surveillance, I figure out her husband's out of town every week until Thursday night about eleven-thirty. Late summer nights allow me to sit with the car windows open. If I hear any approaching vehicles, I leave right away. If anyone spots me, the plan won't work. All it'll take is one nosy do-gooder, one patrolling police officer, and any story I produce won't matter. After her death, someone will remember "that car" or "that lady" in the area recently. I never see joggers or police.

I choose Thursday evening, so she'll be found soon after death and not to risk any evidence loss due to decomposition or a change of weather. Just as predicted for late summer, not a drop of rain fell. The air conditioner runs constantly. Most importantly, there are no dogs to alert my arrival. She'll never hear a thing until I ring the doorbell.

Kacy arrives home from work around seven. By the time I park one block over, she'll have already eaten dinner standing at the kitchen counter. Then she'll walk around the bar and pour her first drink. Flickering light from the television illuminates the living room. Kurt's old boots clomp up the pebbled walk in a nervous gait. I pause making sure my hair is secure in the tight bun. Dressed in a makeshift uniform to perform an unthinkable task, I feel dowdy and unattractive. The cotton jeans and T-shirt I purchased with cash at the Goodwill store. I press the doorbell with my knuckle. She's surprised to see me. We hadn't laid eyes on each other since our last argument many years ago.

The front door cracks open with a brass swag between us. "Kacy?"

"Yes?" Maybe she doesn't recognize me in this costume. "Megan? Is that you?" The door closes the chain slides and then is reopened. "It's been so long! What are you doing here?"

"My new husband and I are considering a lot, right over there." I point at no particular lot in the vast open terrain of the new subdivision. "I spotted you in the yard a couple of days ago. I wanted to stop, but Mike said we just didn't have the time."

"Well! How nice." A high pitch tone accompanies a condescending smile with her false excitement. The pure shock of seeing me at her door brings a flush to her cheeks and infuriates me.

Why do Kacy and Missy get to have normal lives? How come Kurt chose to destroy my life and not one of theirs? It's not fair that they've found happiness and remarried, living the life I deserve. The life I worked so hard for. Kurt didn't just steal my future, he crushed it. Seeing Kacy surrounded by the symbolic spoils of my destruction steels me.

Steadfastly planted on her porch, my presence confronts her with two options. Invite me to enter or not. I hope she chooses the easy one and saves me the trouble of forcing my way in.

"Can you come in and visit?" Kacy hesitates and stretches her neck, perhaps hoping to see a companion in a waiting vehicle to cart me away. Appearing disappointed, but unable to rescind her invitation, she steps back and allows her killer into her home. "Don't just stand there in the heat. It's so good to see you after all this time."

Consistent with the Kacy I remember, lying through her teeth so easily she even convinces herself. She walks to the bar leaving me to close the door. The marble floor of the foyer opens into an expansive living room. She lifts a bottle of Jack Daniels and clinks it against the glass. Her hand shakes as she raises it to drink. She seems to forget her manners and swallows before offering me one.

Ornate, almost gaudy furniture rests on Persian rugs. Now inside the fishbowl, I absorb the ambience of her temporary mausoleum. The laugh track from *Seinfeld* intermittently blares from the television. Cross timbers span the vaulted ceiling and bookshelves wrap around the borders of the room, with nary a book in sight. The shelves are loaded with collections of elaborate Fabergé eggs and cherub-faced Hummel figurines. A fireplace centered on the west wall sustains a colossal hearth and staggered framed photos nest on the mantle.

"Oh, I'm sorry. Would you like a drink?" Another bottle-to-glass note rings out prior to a wobbly amber trickle.

Her nervousness at my presence bolsters my confidence even though I recognize her evening routine of throwing back a few. It's not my appearance that prompts her shots of whiskey. I don't know why Kacy drinks and I don't care. I can't care. I can't think about her problems. They'll be over soon enough. The other me might care, but the me here now... can't. I must keep numb, visualize my actions as robotic.

"No, I really don't have much time." A rush of blood shoots to my head and my heart wants to leap to my throat. I walk past her and peer into the dining room. Paintings contained in garish frames span the walls. Each canvas is illuminated with an oblong lamp mounted above.

Alcohol will calm my anxiety afterwards. If I can just get through this... push away the unbearable feeling of doubt inside me. While her back is to me, I pull the loaded syringe from my pocket and conceal it in my sweating palm.

"I just wanted to drop by and let you in on the good news that we're going to be neighbors, again." I say it with a smile, hoping she can't detect the trembling in my voice. A high back chintz-covered chair provides a firm seat for me. Kacy stands across the coffee table, seeming to size up my true intentions, then takes a seat on the far end of the sofa. I stammer for words, my voice trembling. "Remember when we lived in the same apartment complex? Wow! How long ago was that? Fifteen? No, wait, jeeze, it must've been *sixteen* years ago. Dougy and Ian were just two or three, and I was pregnant with Connor."

She combs a hand through her hair. "Why are you really here, Megan? And don't give this bullshit of being neighbors. Has Kurt turned up?" *I have to act fast.*

"Well, really I just wanted to say hi, but should be going." I lift myself from the chair and pass in front of her pretending to lose my balance. With my right hand I stab the needle into her thigh injecting the liquid. In her reaction to the pain, she pushes hard at me. I lose balance and fall to the floor butt-first.

"What... what the hell?" Furious, she leans forward, crashing the glass on the edge of the coffee table. A small amount of the whiskey sloshes out. She sets the glass upright and rubs the injection site.

Seeing the syringe in my hand she reaches for the phone, but only manages to knock it off the hook. I jump up, grab her shoulders, and push her down on the couch straddling her hips. With her wrists pinned under my thighs, I lock her legs down and hook my feet on top of her shins. Her body tenses, and she jerks from side to side. Is the insulin doing this or is she fighting my hold on her?

I know if I hold still and wait, her strength will recede. Her speech unintelligible, she begins to sweat and shake hysterically. I see from the puzzled look on her face she's trying hard to understand what's happening and why. From the research I've done, I know I could give her some juice or candy and revive her, but I won't. Her confused expression pleads for an answer, but her lips don't move. When the eyes roll back I look away.

Why is it taking so long?

Television voices make no sense. I notice the brown cords that hang behind the paintings in the dining room. They reemerge and then terminate into electrical outlets. How tacky! Why would she spend so much time and money to beautify her home, but overlook such a blatant display of inferior decorating? *No resistance. Hold still a little longer.* The smallest Fabergé egg draws my attention as I clutch her shoulders. The blue façade supports an intricate pattern of gold rope and the broadest surface rests on a bronze base with tiny feet. I remain astride her unmoving form for a couple of minutes after the struggling stops. Now for the most important part of the plan. This is what I rehearsed. I talk myself through it: Get up slowly and walk to the front door, open it, and retrieve the bag, place it on the marble floor at the entrance. With the door closed and locked, I take the rope from the bag and put on a pair of leather gloves. I tie one end into a loop and fling it over one of the rafters, then tighten the noose around her neck.

I carry one of the newly upholstered chairs from the dining room and place it under the rope. I wrestle to lift her limp body off the sofa and position her in the chair, and then pull on the rope until it's taut. The other end of the rope I attach to the clothes rack in the living room coat closet. I decided to use this or perhaps a doorknob if the rack wasn't strong enough to support her. I've seen a lot people who accidently committed suicide by hanging themselves from closet racks and door knobs. They only intended to heighten sexual arousal by temporally cutting off the oxygen to the brain, a new phenomenon labeled "autoerotica."

I lift her butt and place a couple of cushions from the sofa under her. Then I return to the closet and pull the rope tight again. The next time I'm able to get her on to her knees. She's much heavier than I anticipated. To prevent the rope from slipping, I secure it under my heel and continue the exercise of lifting her and pulling the excess rope taut behind me. Whack! Just as the rope supports her entire weight it slides from under my boot. A stretch of it skims up the middle of my back, wadding up my shirt. I grip the rope and freeze, bearing her weight and holding my balance as the rope gouges a crevice along my vertebra. Kacy's head flops back to rest on my shoulder.

Should I abort the mission? Literally drop it all and walk away? My back is on fire. No, Megan, breathe… just breathe.

Lungs full, I give one long tug, lifting the carcass high. I walk backward, taking up the slack in the rope as I pull until her feet dangle at the edge of the chair. My sleeve serves to mop the sweat from my forehead after I tie off the rope.

With the cushions fluffed and arranged alongside the others on the couch, I wipe down everything I may have touched without the gloves. A small piece of wood from the rafter broke loose when the rope slipped and fell to the floor. I leave it where it lay. The syringe safely tucked in the bag, I walk outside, light a cigarette, step into the flowerbed, and twist a boot in the dirt. I flick the ashes and return to the living room, minding each step. A small amount of dirt transfers onto the tile floor and none is visible on the carpet. I proceed to the lifeless body now dangling in midair. Urine drips from her toes wetting the fabric below them. Through the thin film of liquid, I locate the injection mark inside her thigh and burn it with the fire. The skin sizzles and smells of bacon. I turn the lock on the door, close it, and flip more ashes in the dirt. My boot smashes a cigarette butt I'd taken from Kurt's ashtray into the moist soil between two boxwoods planted along the walkway. I discard another remnant of Kurt's ashtray on the street, stuff the gloves in the bag, and walk across the street through the construction site toward my car leaving boot prints. In the desolate night I lean on the car and crush the fire out on the bottom of a boot. I pull them off, setting them in the bag beside the tiny blue egg and zip it shut, then open the trunk and lay the bag inside. I put the extinguished cigarette butt in the ashtray and drive away, recalling my every move.

The whole thing went just as planned. I wore cotton clothes that don't generally shed and didn't take one step out of the living room. Everything possibly touched was wiped clean. I parked on concrete with no mud or dirt to reveal a tire tread pattern and took a path that, come daylight, would be driven on at least a dozen times by emergency vehicles... and utility trucks unloading construction workers.

My gloves, the syringe with cap, the boots, and my smoke butt are all with me. Nothing left behind. My hair was tightly secured. Other than sloughing off a few skin cells, I didn't leave anything that could tie me to this crime.

Kurt is waiting for me, his alibi, to arrive. The darkness swallows me and the white lines whip past in rhythm as I prepare a plausible story and retrace each step of this evening. In a few hours, I'll return with my only opportunity to correct any mistake I made. The unanticipated wood chip on the floor will lead Sam to look for abrasions, to the rafter, and her neck. If she hung herself, she wouldn't have hoisted the rope so many times. The ashes, the footwear impressions, and the dirt I left on the tile are easy enough to spot, but nondescript as far as evidence goes. The boots were an old pair Kurt had left behind all those years ago. We bought identical grey Justin Ropers at the outlet store. Wearing almost the same size, he had taken mine by mistake. I didn't throw his out because, with thick socks, they fit okay for dirty work.

Once I arrive and am positive I didn't leave a shred of unplanned evidence, I let the last couple of hours dissolve into the twisted passion of hate expressed as sex. We lay in bed and I share stories of my sexcapades in the years since we've been apart. He wants to hear all the details and doesn't seem to care who I've had sex with. He also doesn't contribute much of his history to the discussion.

"What happened to you? You're so different. I'm just wondering... where'd you learn so much?" He walks to the other room, returning with a lit cigarette. "Not that I'm complaining." He offers it to me. I take a slow drag and explain after he left I did a lot of growing up.

"Well you know, I married Glynn when I was young. I didn't know anything about sex. You taught me more while we were together than I ever learned from him."

"How come you're not with somebody now? Why didn't you get married again?" He takes the cigarette.

"I tried dating, but it just wasn't for me. I really don't want to answer to anyone. Since you left, I guess I kind of just set out to learn what I wanted. I really opened up sexually and discovered I like pretty much everything. I became rather uninhibited and learned to enjoy sex for what it is, but I didn't want any kind of commitment. My life seemed like a constant thread of sex... men, women and men, it didn't matter to me, as long as I was having fun and nobody got hurt." I stretch the truth for Kurt's entertainment... and to keep his interest while I get enough alcohol in me to mask the tears of rage surfacing.

I tell him about a couple I'd met in a bar at happy hour one night. "The husband, a very handsome man, approached the table where I was sitting with coworkers and offered to buy me a drink. When I accepted, he asked if I'd join him and his wife at their table. Maybe it was the combination of the music, the amount of alcohol I'd already consumed, and a twinkle in his eye intrigued me enough to agree. I lied to my friends. I said they were old friends I hadn't seen in a while. It wasn't out of character for me to leave with a man I'd just met but leaving with a couple might cause them to talk. Conversation among the three of us rapidly turned sexual. It seemed they both found me attractive and wanted me to be part of their *ménage à trois* fantasy."

His undivided attention prompts me to take a long pause. Kurt laps up the juicy details. "So, what'd ya do?"

"I followed them to their house, a huge house over by the country club. We talked awhile and I drank more wine, and then Janet came up behind me and slid her hand up under my blouse and grabbed my breast. The surprise of her touch sent goose bumps down my hips straight to my toes." Remembering the taboo situation made me wet. I wiggle and sit up tall on the bed. "Her husband, George, moved close and started kissing me. I was sandwiched between them. Hands were all over me, on my breasts and down my pants. Before I realized it, I was standing naked between the two of them." Kurt rubs his crotch.

"Man, some guys have all the luck. Go on. What happened next?" he demands.

I brush my hair back with my palms and continue. "I was the center of attention for these two. Once we were on the bed they devoured me, like an all-you-can-eat buffet. He was between my legs and she was caressing and sucking my breast. I'd never been naked with a woman before so... I grabbed a handful..." I squeeze my own breast, disappointed with the comparison.

Kurt moans. "So, were her tits big or small?"

"Her boobs were perfect." I hold my hands out at my chest and show him the underside of her breasts fit in my cupped palms.

Kacy's eyes roll back, eyelids fluttering, a disturbing vision. Talk louder and faster, Megan. Fight the urge to scream.

"They were 'artificially enhanced' and didn't have one bit of sag. We wrestled around on their bed for what seemed hours.

They put on at first like it was all new for them too, but I don't think it was their first rodeo. And their bed, you wouldn't believe this bed. It was huge, king-sized, with posts and velvet drapes like in a castle."

Kurt doesn't need to know anything more about George and Janet or our "friendship" that continued long after the first encounter. They introduced me to a lifestyle I'd only heard of in derogatory jokes—"swingers." On my child-free weekends, I experienced the taboo world of sexual freedom. Occasionally, a spontaneous orgy would occur at a "couples" party or a lifestyle club. The mornings that followed brought thoughts of regret. Then, with another invitation from George or Janet, I'd push aside the remorse, put on a skimpy dress and tall heels, and join them again. I came a long way in a short time from the Southern Baptist, guilt-burdened girl my grandmother bestowed upon me. Once I grew accustomed to the lifestyle, the excitement waned. I couldn't let my studies suffer, so I backed off and began to visit less often.

Kurt pushes me to the bed and fucks me hard. Is he trying to prove he can satisfy me as much as George and Janet had or is he just turned on by my story? I squeeze my eyes tight, but I can't replace the vision of Kacy's agonized expression with another. Kurt grunts, and with each thrust, the friction provides me enough distraction to escape into his stimulating rhythm. I remind myself to enjoy it... for what it is, the means to an end... sex.

12:30, finally in the driveway at home, Connor's in bed and Ian is lying on the couch asleep with the Atari remote still in his hand. These are the last few days of his childhood to enjoy the games of a boy before we head to Florida State next week.

I crawl in bed to cry the familiar tears of frustration and rage. My hour of sleep is fitful, knowing I have to do it again. When the phone rings at 2:00, I know who, what, when, where, and how. My body shakes at another moment of doubt. Can I return there? I take a deep breath and put one foot in front of the other. Hopefully, with only a short nap, my apprehension will appear as sleep deprivation.

23

THURSDAY, OCTOBER 20, 1994

*C*rime novels claim second murders are always easier than the first. Up until now I might have believed it to be true, given the first didn't happen by accident or in the heat of passion. Those happen quickly. Cold, calculated murders are different. Preparation for the first was much less difficult than this one. The goal was to accomplish both murders within a month, but it wasn't possible. To get them onto Kurt quickly I felt I had to tell Sam about my connection to Kacy through Kurt soon after her murder. But now so much time has passed since her death, I might be rushing Missy's. Extra planning, attention to detail, with a lot of luck, and hopefully I won't forget anything. Hap's concern worries me though; he's threatening to put a bodyguard with me. If he does, I'll never be able to pull this off.

Missy lives in a very busy neighborhood. Matthew, Kurt and Missy's eleven-year-old son, lives with her, her new husband Larry, and his son Joey. The constant stream of kids in and around their house is a huge obstacle to overcome and requires enough time to prepare a failsafe plan. It's mid-fall, the final days of another warm Texas October. The murder will have to occur while the kids are in school. This means making contact with Missy in broad daylight, without the cover of darkness or the seclusion of an entire region under construction.

The area consists of typical one-story/three-bedroom/two-bath structures. Alleys provide access to rear-entry garages. The main thoroughfares run in a general north-south grid making it difficult to cruise the vicinity. With no traffic during the day, "blending in" is impossible. The mail carrier delivers every day around lunchtime. From the street, the neighborhood appears deserted; except for demonic jack-o-lanterns peering from porches and low thread-count ghosts suspended from a hackberry tree.

Missy's bright yellow Mustang allows me to observe her comings and goings from the alley at a considerable distance. She takes the boys to school and runs short errands every weekday morning. Her bouncy steps and petite figure portray a look much more youthful than her thirty-five years. Positioned at the far end of the school yard, I follow as she picks them up in the afternoon. After she drops them in front of the house, she sets off for work at the children's hospital. She's a nurse. I'm reminded yet again how another of Kurt's conquests not only survived his wrath but prospered in the wake of it.

I'm unsure how to approach her. Every day I rack my brain, each day more frustrating than the last. How can I get her to let me in her home and make her feel at ease? She won't just let me in. Missy never liked me. She blamed me for the drastic drop in child support a judge ordered years ago. I heard she believed somehow, I was the reason for Kurt leaving, causing the halt of child support payments altogether. One Friday, just when I'm about to lose hope, I drive down her street and see a U-Haul truck backed into the yard of the house next door and a Century 21 Realty sign in the yard. A vacant house next door would be very helpful. I need to get inside her house unseen during the day. With just a few more details to work out, hope is restored.

I worked a crime scene in a nearby city that gave me an idea for the way in. A woman had forced her loser boyfriend to move out of her house. When he began to threaten and harass her, her mother moved in so she wouldn't be alone until she could get the house sold. One day as the mother worked in the back yard, she left the rear entry garage door open. With the privacy of the alley, the ex-boyfriend walked into the garage unnoticed. He hid in the house. We never knew if the mother discovered his hiding place or if he snuck up on her before he stabbed her to death. The intruder left her to bleed out in the master bathroom. Sam and I deduced after he closed the garage door, he ate a sandwich and watched television while he waited for the daughter to return from work. Confronted in the laundry room, he shot her in the face. He was caught driving her car… he left his bicycle in her garage. He might have been lucky up to that point, but he wasn't very smart. The saddest part is she lived. I remember thinking that day how grateful I was that Kurt's actions hadn't produced horrific consequences on anyone but me.

When the day for Missy's death arrives, I'm tired. I hadn't planned for the trailer park crime scene in the middle of the night. My exhaustion helps bury my emotions. The preparation and elimination of obstacles, both real and emotional, are accomplished. It's just another repulsive job that I must do… again, and if I stick to the plan I can do it.

From the parking lot at the 7-Eleven on the corner near Missy's neighborhood, I watch as the yellow Mustang drives past. She's taking the boys to school. I know I have about ten minutes before she returns. I drive down her street, no one in sight. The jack-o-lanterns stare at me with jagged grins as a cardboard witch riding a broom twists in the breeze.

I drive to my predetermined spot a couple of blocks over. I park between a dumpster and dilapidated fence. I position a backpack stuffed with towels on my front side. Wearing the same jeans I'd worn to Kacy's, I tie my hair up in a tight coil and tuck it up under a dirty old maroon Peterbilt cap I'd found and zip up a big sweatshirt jacket over my backpack. Wearing Kurt's clunky boots and no makeup, I hop on the bike and peddle around, my belly making me resemble a pudgy man. Most of the view for the distance I travel up the alley is obstructed by six-foot stockade fences. I rest the bicycle inside the back yard of the vacant house next door, put on the gloves, and carefully place the loaded syringe in the pocket of the fleece jacket. I stash the backpack between the bicycle and the fence and crouch between the houses. Hidden from view, I drop one of Kurt's cigarette butts in the freshly watered bare lawn and press it down with my toe.

The hum of the garage door opener warns of her arrival. Making sure I'm out of sight, I take a few deep breaths—eyes closed, my heartbeat slows. I gear up for what I know is ahead. To be done with this task and finally get some sleep is the pressing goal.

A distinct low rumble of the Mustang's engine grows closer. The car pulls to the far right in the garage. I position myself low enough to enter and hide between the rear of the car and the wall. Missy turns off the ignition, opens the car door then closes it with a thud. I peer through the windows and watch long, chemically treated blond hair sway against her pale bare shoulders. She's barefoot and steps around the grease spot lying in her path. Cut-off blue jean shorts and a red ribbed tank top compliment her tiny frame. She could easily be mistaken for a teenager from behind. She pushes a button and the garage door descends. I breathe in the fumes and sit on the cold concrete floor feeling the heat from the exhaust pipe. I wait. Click, the light dims, then goes off.

Sitting in the dark, my mind fills with the sensations I felt just hours ago with Tyler. Our slippery, sweaty bodies tangled together in constant motion. The contrasting colors and physical mass easily distinguishing male from female, black from white. I know a future with Tyler isn't possible. Even without the preju-dices in this large, backwater town, I'll never feel smart enough, pretty enough, or young enough.

Barely audible television sounds and plumbing noises help

me track her movements. I wait a few more minutes for her to get comfortable. Then I walk across the garage, make a purposeful step in the oil patch, and open the door into the house. I ease into the utility room and leave the door ajar. Unsure of the floor plan, I poke my head from the laundry room and scan the area. I see her crossed legs on the overstuffed teal saddleback sofa, facing the TV. A lampshade on the end table blocks her view of me. I rock back on my heels, take another calming breath, and pluck a small towel from a basket on top of the dryer.

The simplicity of this and my lack of anxiety scares me. Have I overlooked something, or does it really get easier to kill? I pull the syringe from my pocket, remove the cap, and conceal it with the towel. I walk toward her. Eye to eye, less than a foot away, she stands up, unable to register why I'm here, in her house, uninvited. In her moment of confusion, I lunge toward her and pierce her thigh with a thrust that injects the insulin. Missy flinches and takes a few steps back.

"You fucking bitch. What the hell are you doing?" She picks up the gold Trimline phone and stares at it. She seems unable to focus on the keypad. The insulin's reaction is quick, just as it was with Kacy. She drops to the sofa. The receiver falls to the floor and she grabs her head with both hands. I bend over, pick up the phone with the dishtowel, and place it back on the base.

In a concerned mocking tone, I ask, "What's wrong, Missy?"

"You… fucking bitch… stuck me… in my leg." Missy's speech is thick. She pinches her thigh where I jabbed the needle. Standing, she stumbles and falls back to the couch. I wrap my arm around her small waist and lift her to her feet. We walk toward the garage with me steadily prodding her wobbly gait.

She sweats and complains, "My head hurts."

I couldn't resist telling her what I didn't have the courage to tell Kacy. "Well, you're gettin' what you deserve! You were a pain in my ass for years!"

An effort to swing at me results in heavy arms scarcely

moving. As we round the refrigerator, her right hand flops toward the butcher block knife set on the counter. I prevent her from reaching a knife, but her bracelet catches on the strike plate of the doorjamb. Elastic stretches to beyond its strength and breaks, flinging small glass beads across the room.

Her words slur. "Where are…?"

"We're just going to your beautiful car, for a little nap." A few green beads crunch beneath the clunky boots.

I push open the door with the towel. The vibrant car is quite visible at the far side of the dark garage. We cross the threshold and I flip on the light. After taking a few shuffled steps toward the car, Missy's legs give way. I finagle my arm under her knees and cradle her. She's deadweight heavy, but not impossible to lift.

I was surprised when I discovered she still owns the classic Mustang. Missy's father gave her the perfectly restored car for her sixteenth birthday. I always assumed she treasures the car because it was the last gift her father gave her. He died shortly afterward. Watching her drive it these past weeks, I think how profound that she'll take her last few breaths in it.

There are no other vehicles in the garage, a couple of bicycles, a lawnmower, and boxes of toys stashed on racks. I carry her to the car and open the driver's door, lean over and tip her head in first. Her butt lands hard in the driver's seat. I lay her waist gently over the black vinyl console and let her head and shoulders flop into the passenger's seat.

Back inside, I find her purse and locate the keys. I freely traipse through the dining room and back down the short hallway—crunch, crunch—the beads crack and pop. Returning to the garage I make sure to walk in the grease spot again. Her purse falls on the garage floor next to the open car door and items spill haphazardly. I lean over her, put the key in the ignition, and start the engine. The radio, tuned to an oldies station, is so appropriate. Patsy Cline belts out Crazy.

I back out of the car, careful not to dislodge my hat. Missy's body begins to convulse. The twitching is disturbing to see, but I watch anyway. Just like Kacy, all I need to do to save her now is put a little sugar under her tongue. I won't. I can't. As I watch, I light a cigarette and suck a long draw causing the fire to lengthen and burn hot.

The melancholic words Patsy sings seem so appropriate after what Kurt has done to me.

In a few hours, *Sympathy for the Devil* will wash the looping lyrics of *Crazy* from my head.

A small drop of blood sits on her thigh where the needle punctured the skin. I push the fire on it and the hiss and aroma of cooked meat camouflage the wound. The shaking of her body lessens as her respiration increases. The miserable words of the song drone.

I turn my back, knowing death will come quickly now. She'll take shallow breaths for a few minutes after her body stops convulsing. The carbon monoxide will fill her lungs, and she'll go to sleep forever.

The footprints left by the boots look unplanned and absent-mindedly track across the garage and fade onto the hallway linoleum floor. I flick ashes in one, balance on one foot, stub the fire out on the sole of the boot and put the butt in my pocket.

"That was Patsy Cline singin' Willie Nelson's *Crazy*," the DJ announces in an exaggerated voice. Huh! You learn something new every day. I didn't know Willie Nelson wrote that song!

a little light-headed, I walk through the dining room into the kitchen. The television suppresses the engine's noise. I go out the French door into the backyard and through a wooden gate that leads to the driveway. The closed garage door mutes the deep rumbling of the engine. I enter the adjacent gate, push it closed, and loosen the backpack from the bicycle leaning against the fence. Methodical movements, just as rehearsed. With a few deep breaths I steady myself, shed the gloves, return the bag to its previous position, and sprinkle in a few green glass beads. I roll the bike into the alley and ride back to my car. After removing the front wheel, I put it, the backpack, and the carcass of the bicycle in the trunk. Finally done! Really done. Enough killing! All that's left to do now is get much-needed rest and plant a few more seeds to implicate Kurt.

We're working with a skeleton crew this week. Many of my coworkers are at a conference this week. I know I'll be called to this scene in a few hours. Sleep-deprived and drained, I return home to find the only indication Tyler's been here, an empty burrow of bed linens. My heart shares a similar vacant tunnel where warmth and purity once rested comfortably. Whatever remaining innocence resided there died today, with Missy.

Kurt's disappearance robbed the boys of their father so many years ago. Now I've taken their mothers, and even though he's returned, soon their father... forever. I hardly feel human anymore. The coolness of the sheets proves I still possess some feeling. The void in my soul floods with sadness, suffocating me into unconsciousness.

IN THE THREE weeks before my appointment with Dr. Mann, I work hard to block out the revulsion of what I've done and resume normalcy. If I bury it deep enough, it'll be easier to act like it never happened. I clean the house, bathe the dogs, and even have my mother over for dinner with Connor and me.

During the interview, I pass along the necessary information, making sure she knows Kurt ran out on his children and me to avoid going to jail and he was a suspect in the Dena Morgan murder. For days after the interview, I replay and evaluate every word I remember from our conversation. Maybe I should've told her Kurt was more violent, especially when I mentioned his comments that his exes would be better off dead. That he threw things and ranted over their existence in his world. Telling her of Jules's warning was good, and the foreboding I ignored... because I loved Kurt so much.

I shouldn't have told her that Hap was questioned in Dena's murder or about the two of hearts. Were her questions meant to test me? Did I say more or reveal any part of my role in Kacy's and Missy's deaths with my silent response to rhetorical questions? Was she patronizing me? And how dare she ask about my father! What does my relationship with my father have to do with Kurt killing his exes? There is the one question I can't provide an answer for, why? Why would Kurt come back after six years? Just to kill two women so far in his past? Does this generate doubt of his guilt?

Concerned looks greet me when I return to work. I sense my

story has spread to everyone on Kurt's trail and anyone else interested in entertaining gossip at my expense. I see it in their eyes. As the weeks pass and the holidays approach, my paranoia grows. I can't continue to visit the cabin. What if Hap finds out about it? Finding excuses not to see Kurt are running thin, along with my desire to be with him.

The week before Thanksgiving, Kurt disappears and Jackie shows up on my doorstep. What if all I've done is for nothing? If he couldn't be found for six years, can they find him now that he's wanted for two murders? No one knows his new name. How can I let them know? I could lead them to the cabin, but first I'll need to remove any trace I've been there and that won't be easy with Jackie at my heels.

25

"Mom, Mom!" Ian waves an arm. He stands a good foot above others de-boarding the plane.

"There he is! Mom, look, there." Connor points and tugs at my coat sleeve.

Ian lifts me from the ground in a hug, stirring the mom gene. I need to have him home. Spending so little time with the two of them before their flight for Denver leaves me longing for a traditional Thanksgiving dinner. I want my life back in order, our lives the way we were six months ago, prior to the July heat igniting that two of hearts in a parking lot.

"Are you excited about getting some time away from school to go see your Dad and ski?" The three of us lock elbows and stroll down the corridor.

"I'm more excited to go skiing than to see my Dad."

"Ian!" My slap at his arm is muffled by his heavy coat.

"It's true, Mom." Connor chimes in. "We'd much rather be there with you than Dad. He stays drunk all the time." Ian nudges an elbow into his side.

I sweep around in front, stopping them. "Promise me—look at me, both of you, look straight here." I point to my eyes and bob back and forth to theirs. "Promise me you will not get in the car and let him drive if he's been drinking. Promise me."

Exaggerating my command, both of them place a nose within inches of mine. "It's okay, Mom, don't worry," Ian assures me. "Since he got arrested for driving drunk, he makes Callie or me drive everywhere."

Somewhat relieved, I watch until their plane pulls away from the gate, headed for the tarmac. Lonesome and sad, I drive home and spend the Thanksgiving holidays depressed and scared. Hap is trapped with family. He calls to check on me a couple of times.

Mine and Kurt's wedding anniversary falls on the Friday after Thanksgiving, and Kurt leaves a broken message on my answering machine. Although it agitates me, I'm relieved to know he hasn't pulled another vanishing act and am thankful the answering machine is in my bedroom out of Jackie's earshot. "I just need some air... taking a little road trip... I'll be back after Christmas, plan on New Year's Eve together. Oh yeah, I almost forgot, Happy Anniversary! Next year we'll spend it together, I promise."

What's he up to? Is he with the family he deserted to come back here? Does he know what I've done? Has he told the police what I'm doing? What if they're watching *me* and just pretending to be looking for him? Is Jackie a spy?

Panic won't help, Megan. You're just being paranoid. Nobody knows. You've covered all the bases. You're safe. It's over. You have the key and the paperwork for the bank. There's one thing left to do.

Relieved to know he hasn't disappeared, I take advantage of his time away. As soon as Jackie gets in the shower the next morning, I head for the lake house. I park behind tall hedges to the west of the house and sling the pack over my shoulder. Glass beads in the boots jostle in rhythm with my steps toward the boathouse. The water level is low. There's no sign of any boats on the lake in front of the cabin. A cold breeze skates across the water as I climb up the weathered boards. The top plank gives way under my weight, I grab the doorframe and pull myself into the interior of the structure, lessening the possibility of someone spotting me. The building sways with the wind. I hurry, knowing my only opportunity to leave the items collected from Kacy's and Missy's has to be fast.

The evidence may never be revealed if I hide it too well or if the clues I placed at the scenes go unnoticed. I hold out hope the rickety old structure won't collapse into the lake before this proof of Kurt's guilt is discovered. I wrap the blue egg from Kacy's collection in Missy's kitchen towel and stuff the bundle in the right boot. Curling the brim of the Peterbilt cap as I'd seen Kurt do so many times, I slide it into the left boot and set the pair behind a pile of tattered old lifejackets in the corner. Taking a few steps back and sideways, I make sure they look hidden, but remain visible. God, I hope they're found.

The thud of a car door resonates... Shit! Carefully, I tiptoe dockside for a look. The only car I see is mine and no one's near it. Shit! Is it Kurt? Maybe it's a taxi bringing Kurt back from wherever the hell he went? I climb down the ladder trusting no one will see me and try to think how to explain my presence to Kurt. The screen creaks as I step up to the back porch and peer in the window. It's not Kurt. The house is empty. The noise of crunching gravel carries to the backyard. I leap from the porch and dart through the flower beds alongside the house just in time to see the tail end of a white car in a cloud of dust. It wasn't a taxi. Whoever it was is gone now, allowing me to carry through with my plans to rid the house of any telltale signs I'd been here in the last few years.

Did the person in the white car see me or my car? If they did, there's nothing you can do about it, Megan. All you can do now is wait. Wait for Kurt to be found and arrested, then it'll all be over. You'll have your life back.

I wish I could be the proverbial fly on the wall when they find him. To see the look in his eyes when all his plans are plucked from his grasp would be the greatest reward. I want him to realize I'm the one responsible for sending him straight to the hell he thought he'd avoided.

I wait through Christmas, not really expecting his arrest after the message he left.

～

DESPITE THE RISK for me to return to the cabin for New Year's Eve, I know these will be my last moments with Kurt. I need to stay close to assure myself that he doesn't suspect anything and being in his presence knowing what is about to befall him is an adrenalin rush I can't resist. They'll catch him soon.

To escape Jackie on New Year's Eve, I falsely confess of a tradition to spend the holiday with a certain "friend."

"I don't know, Megan. Hap'll kill me if he finds out," she whines.

"He'll never know. Connor and Ian will still be in Colorado and they're the only ones who could give it away," I beg. "After all, I have covered for you a couple of times. You owe me." Perhaps she's difficult at first, but then folds easily because she thinks I'll be with Hap.

"Besides, it's been months since Missy's death and nothing. Maybe Kurt crawled back under the rock he called home for so long. I'll be careful."

Kurt and I spend New Year's Eve together in bed surrounded by candles. He's decorated the cabin with streamers and prepared an array of my favorite foods, sweet pears, dark chocolate, and Regiano cheese. With playful seduction we feed each other like we did on our honeymoon and Valentine's, and sip champagne. An ease settles over me, comfortable and laughing, but sad, very sad. A banner over the fireplace announces the arrival of 1995 in black and gold. Memories of a happier time draped in mourning. "Just think, we're only five years from the turn of a century."

I leave him certain the end will come soon. Wintry weather

sets in and the whole world seems frozen. Nothing happens. I concentrate on work and wait. Wait for Hap to find Kurt.

I'm shocked to see Kurt and April at the Stock Show. Why was he with her? Was he seeing her all along? I wonder if my decision to spare her was a wise one. To see her floating in the lake was such a shock. I'm still puzzled. I didn't take her life. Did I? Have I lost my grip on reality?

You're okay Megan. Don't question your sanity or your motives. Stand strong, be strong, mentally and physically strong.

But why would Kurt kill her? Did he? Was Kurt really capable of murder? A strange thought to consider now and a point made moot with his arrest. After my visit to the jail, I wonder was Kurt preparing April to retrieve the money from its hiding place in case someone was watching, waiting for him to reveal the hiding place. I retrieve the key from the box, place it on a chain and wear it around my neck, the talisman of my dilemma.

In the weeks following Kurt's arrest, I've come to regret my arrogant visit to the jail. The basic rule of murder is keep your mouth shut. I know that. I also know my oh-so-subtle confession was a huge mistake. I should've killed him when I had the chance. Shortly afterward, I received proof I should've left it alone: a letter from Kurt.

MEGAN,

YOU TOLD me you loved me more than you ever thought you could love anyone. I miss your touch. Every day I close my eyes to remember your smell and the giggles in my ear when I kiss your neck. What I wouldn't do for another chance. Our love will survive in this lifetime to be what was intended so long ago when our souls first met.

I'm so sorry I screwed it up this time. Nothing's ever hurt me more than watching you leave. I know now how you must have felt when I left you. I'm sorry, I can't stand this isolation from you. Please come see me. I need you to know our love still exists.

LOVE,

Kurt

P.S. Did you find the key?

I FOUND myself wanting to believe his apology, almost feeling sorry for him and regretting what I'd done, until the postscript. Kurt might have figured it out eventually, but without my confirmation there was doubt. Foolishly, my choice to satisfy the hunger of seeing his face as he realized I did this to him may cause it all to crash down around me. On second thought, he did tell me about the key.

Within a month, another letter expressing desperation came.

MEGAN,

WE CAN WALK AWAY *from this mess. You know what I mean. Let's pick up the pieces and move on, get past this. Please don't stay away from me too long. This place is horrible. I'll go crazy if I stay here much longer.*

I need you and I'm scared you've forgotten our souls' journey together is beyond our control. I don't understand how you could leave me in here.

I have no one, even my boys won't come see me or even write me. I trusted you.

COME TO ME,

Kurt

26

*M*onths pass with Kurt in jail, awaiting trial. His letters turn threatening. The first letters I received were taped on an edge, obviously screened before leaving the jail. Then I begin receiving them in sealed envelopes. I can only surmise the lack of inspection tells me he's probably marking them as legal material, off limits. Unsure of the contents and not wanting it traced back to the Fishburn law firm, a secretary slaps a stamp on the envelope bearing my address. Not exactly an illegal act, but definitely an unethical one.

Megan,

This is the last letter before I tell my lawyer everything. I've sat here long enough. If you wanted to pay me back, you have. I've been in here almost a year, let's call it even. What kind of person are you to leave me in here like this after all we've been through? You can't possibly understand how terrible it is here. I trusted you. Have you gone for the money yet? You know where it is, just go get it and get me out, please!

Kurt

I burn the last two letters, but I place the first in the shoebox with mine, salvaged from Kurt's outrage.

Hap and I spend many evenings after work at the Shamrock, a pub not far from the courthouse, where assistant DAs cluster after work. Occasionally someone we know will join us, but mostly we sit alone. Ian comes home occasionally for a day or two with me, then a couple of days with his dad before returning to school. Connor's busy with his girlfriend and the new BMW his dad gave him for Christmas. It seems he's never home.

With the investigation closed, even Jackie isn't around anymore, except with Ed. They've been dating steady since April surfaced almost a year ago. I knew when Tyler stopped calling for impromptu dinners and sex there was another woman. I wasn't prepared for the sting when a coworker told me he'd run into Tyler at Home Depot. "He's engaged to a tall blonde woman, an attorney, matter of fact she looks a lot like you." I suppose he's unsure if he's inflicted enough pain, so he adds, "I hear they're expecting a child."

On the heels of that insult another letter from Kurt arrives.

Megan,

Ok bitch you know I said they'd be better off dead? So will you. I can only assume you've got my money. Get me the fuck out of here. I haven't told my lawyer everything yet, because I'm hoping there's still a chance some of my money is left. If you don't get me out soon I'm going to tell him everything. I don't know how you killed them, Megan, but I know you did. If you don't come see me by the first of March, so help me God, you'll pay for this.

By the way, how was Ireland?

Kurt

I IGNORE HIS LETTERS. I caress the key, but only fantasize about going after the money. It'd be fun to flaunt newfound wealth if Ruby were still alive. Since her death and the arrival of their first annuity checks, my sons don't spend much time at home. With their financial futures guaranteed, I have little use for Kurt's money.

Scared and alone, Hap is all I have anymore. When I'm not with him, I'm home worried. We drink and treat each other to dinner occasionally, or I drink a lot and we eat nothing. We talk of everything, except Kurt and the dead women. He seems to know how vulnerable I am and he keeps the world at bay. I think of telling him about the letters, not confessing to anything, just letting him know how Kurt's trying to manipulate me, but I fear the investigator in Hap will push it beyond the point of no return and I'll lose him too. Without him, I'm unprotected and terrified. Most nights, he sees I make it home okay and lets me fall asleep on his chest as we watch the news on the sofa. Our intimate friendship remains unconsummated.

ONE NIGHT at the bar he presses a topic I wish would flitter away like the ashes of Kurt's letters. "Megan, I know we haven't talked about the murders in a while, but the trial will be starting soon and I want you to know the toxicology results came in yesterday. Did you know they'd sent blood over to the Dallas County lab?" Sometimes they do the work on cases considered sensitive to the law enforcement arena in Fort Worth.

I shook my head. "No. I stay clear of anyone working on Kacy's and Missy's murders. Why?"

"Well, it seems the ol' doc couldn't determine a cause of death for Kacy, seems she was already dead before she was strung up, and our tox lab showed nothing but a little ethanol." Yeah… ninety-proof Jack to be exact, I thought. "So he sent the blood on the three of 'em over to Dallas."

Hap slides his hand under his jacket and lifts a pack of blue Trues from his front shirt pocket. He lights a cigarette and blows the smoke straight up to the ceiling.

"I wish you'd quit... again." I take the cigarette from him and draw from the plastic Tinker Toy-looking filter. "Oh God that's gross! How do you smoke these?" I hand it back to him and hold my empty pint up for the bartender to see. "You want another?" I stand up, tug my skirt back down over my hips with one hand and an empty glass in the other.

"No. I'm good. Megan, sit down." Hap points to my chair.

"They found elevated levels of insulin in Kacy and Missy. They're doing some research now with insulin and the ratio of peptide C... or something, it's far from...." Hap digs his little notebook from his jacket pocket and flips through the pages. "Well, I wrote all this down, but I'm not sure what it means. Even though neither one of them was diabetic... they really can't prove an insulin overdose." His hands are shaking.

I stop mid-step and turn. 'What about April?"

"Nothing. She was strangled." Looking confused, he leans down to make eye contact with me.

"*What?*" I return to my seat and hold the empty glass up again. "Why won't that bartender look this way?"

"Kurt's a diabetic... an insulin-dependent diabetic." He stares at me. "And... and..." The words become unintelligible.

What does he want from me? "Yes, I know."

Hap rubs his shoulder and, even in the low light, I notice he's sweating. "I spoke with Dr. Mann... and you... I want you to... you should know..."

"Hap!" Just as I reach for him, his body stiffens and he crumples to the floor. "Call 911! Somebody, call 911!" I scream. People come from every corner. My mind races to remember CPR as I begin chest compressions.

"Move!" A man pushes me aside and takes over the life-saving measures. I stand by stunned... in shock. *Know what? What should I know?*

I drive to the hospital and sit in the waiting room with some of his fellow officers. Hernandez recognizes Sylvia when she arrives and runs to escort her in and past the waiting room crowd to Hap's bedside.

"That's Hap's wife," another cop said. I know he had no way of knowing, but the words grate my heart.

She doesn't deserve him. Hap wasted a lifetime of love on this emotional vacuum of time and space. No more than useless flesh dependent on others for sustainability.

Sylvia looks quite different than I imagined. She's tall and slender. Thin strawberry-blond hair frames her face. A narrow nose and pale translucent skin give her a fragile, helpless appearance. I always thought she'd be chubby, dark-haired, angry, puckered, and rigid like my mother. Her sweetness commands attention from every occupant in the waiting room. What a victim, poor thing.

Once I know Hap's stable and they're not going to let me see him, I leave for home… alone. I'm not family, and his condition is serious. I'm not allowed in. He needs me more than anyone right now, and I need him. My world is collapsing, and I have no one. I curl up in my closet and cry.

27

THURSDAY, MAY 1, 1996

"Well, after a year and a half, the trial is finally set for the 12th," Tyler says as he crams a folder down in his briefcase and walks quickly. I hold an umbrella high to shelter us both from the rain as we dart across Weatherford Street from the courthouse to the Tandy Center for lunch. "Megan, are you okay? I know you want this to be over. Put this behind you… and get on with your life." He speaks loudly over the heavy traffic. We dodge cars against the light.

The Bass brothers are renovating downtown into the yuppie-pleasing Sundance Square. A new generation of citizens shows appreciation, among the chaos of construction. During the week, the lowly office workers still head for the Tandy Center Mall. We weave through the maze of barricades and puddles of mud into the vestibule between glass doors. Tyler braces the door with his foot and shifts his briefcase to his left hand. "Here, let me get that. How're ya doing? The boys okay?"

"I'm fine. I'm great, we're all doing good." I shake the water from the umbrella.

The Nine West summer sandal display captures my attention, and I wish my worries could return to something as simple as yearning to afford a new pair of shoes. I broke the golden rule of murderers.

"Come on, let's get something to eat." Tyler tugs my elbow and points toward the escalator. I carefully step onto the moving stairs, and my high heels wobble on the grooved surface. One set of escalators crisscrosses the center of an ice rink from the third floor to the first floor. We ride down the one that flanks the east end from the street level to the rink and food court level. "It's Heaven on Ice" is touted on the souvenir postcards for sale. The same postcard touts "park free and ride the world's only free subway." The old Leonard's department store subway delivers tourists and downtown's workforce from remote parking to the city streets via a walk amid an array of stores.

The conglomerate odor is a confusing mixture from the Chinese buffet, Italy by the Sea, and Sonny Bryan's BBQ. We opt for barbecue and plop our plates of brisket and potato salad on one of the few available tables overlooking the ice rink. Tyler perches on a tiny chair and places his briefcase in the one beside him.

"Megan, I talked with Kurt's lawyer Friday morning. You know scaly Mike Fishburn. He won't take a plea." He took the plastic utensils from their cellophane wrapper. "I offered him twenty with no parole. That's damn good for two murders. We could've pushed for death." Potato salad on the fork, he pauses. "He says Kurt is innocent."

I don't respond. *Did Kurt really tell him?* I take another bite of brisket and watch the instructor teaching his young students to skate backwards.

Tyler snaps his fingers in front of my face. "Megan!"

I withdraw from another constant reminder of what I've done, a mother tending to her fussy baby in a stroller. "What?" I turn to face him.

"For a year I've been trying to keep this from going to trial."

I give him my undivided attention. "Because?" *Why is he still saying say two murders?* "Two murders? There were three. And...

if I were you, I would go for the death penalty," I say, unfeeling... numb. "Why haven't you called to see how I'm doing?" I wait for his gaze to meet mine.

"Because... Fishburn is insinuating... his defense is blaming you." He dares me to look away.

"Me?" I hold at attention. *No downcast glance, no nod. Maintain, Megan, just maintain.*

"Yeah, Kurt's claiming you killed Kacy and Missy." Tyler waves his fork at me accusingly. "We can't be seen together. If anyone knew about us I'd be pulled off this case and honestly... Megan, you need me on this!"

"No, you need me, to keep our secret, because this is the biggest case of your career and you're afraid of a scandal, of messing up your parents' plan."

Tyler stabs the meat, turns the fork backwards and pulls the meat with his teeth. "So, what'd you say?"

"What?"

"What did you say to Kurt when you went to the jail to see him?" The pace of his question hit me hard.

"I didn't confess to anything other than how happy it makes me to know he's finally paying for all the crap he put me through. I didn't tell him I killed anyone, and I don't care what he says."

Oh God, he did it. Kurt told Fishburn. My life is over. What will my boys think?

I blow it off. "Let it go to trial. You know you could at least act like you still care about me. We're sitting here together now." I look down and wring the paper napkin. Tyler grabs my wrist tightly.

"You're a witness. I'm talking to one of my witnesses. What's wrong with you? You're not yourself." He lets go of my wrist and I rub it.

"How would you know me lately? I haven't heard from you in months! When were you gonna tell me about your wife and baby? Don't I even matter to you anymore as a friend, if nothing else?" I toss the napkin onto my plate full of food and hang my head, realizing I really do need Tyler. Even though he abandoned me, too.

"I'm sorry, I really shouldn't jump down your throat. It's Hap, he's in the hospital. He's had a heart attack."

I stare at the potato salad on the edge of his plate. "I'm worried. I want to see him, but they won't let me because I'm not family." I feel so isolated and alone. How difficult will it be for me to get to Kurt's money? Where in the hell is the Isle of Man and the Mount Murray Golf Club?

---

*T*he day after my meeting with Tyler, I finally find my way into Hap's room by tagging along with Sam on an official business matter. He's snoring loudly as we enter the room. Wires connected to beeping monitors and flashing lights distract my attention from the green oxygen tube contrasting his grey pallor. He looks so old and I feel so alone.

Waking with a groggy start, he and Sam find comfortable ground outside the seriousness of Hap's condition by trading old-men and cruel-lawyer jokes. Between labored breaths, Sam listens as Hap recalls as much as he can of the incident. I fill in the remaining details. Sam excuses himself, claiming to have some pressing work to get back to at the lab. Reality bites. Sam is a couple of years older than Hap. Maybe he sees himself in that bed soon if he continues to smoke.

"I'll be there soon..." I stay behind. Sam disappears into the hall, leaving the door open behind him.

"Hap! I'm so glad you're okay." My heart leaps that I have a few minutes alone with him. I come to him and lay my head on his chest.

"Well, I'm still alive, darling! Not so much okay as just alive." His hand lands on my head and pulls my hair back, holding it in a mock pony tail. "I need to tell you something." His chest rises and falls as I listen to his deep voice, he squeezes my shoulders. "A story, a long-ago story…" He struggles for a breath. "And I need you to listen." I hear the raspy air in his chest.

"Go… shut the door… I don't have much time, so don't interrupt!" He removes the oxygen tube from his nose.

I help him place a pillow behind his shoulders so he can sit up. "You should rest. I'll come back later."

"I… said don't… interrupt…" He fights for enough breath to get the words out.

"When I was thirteen, a family moved into our neighborhood. They bought the little grocery store up there on 377. You know, over there in Benbrook… I showed you my parents' house one time. You… remember?"

I nodded. "Yes."

"They had a daughter. She was eight or nine… their only child, always… in the store with them, when she wasn't in school. I watched her grow up… into a fine… young woman. Dena started high school the year I was a senior. I thought she was the most beautiful girl I ever met. I don't think she even knew I existed back then." He motions for his cup of water. I hold it as his fingers locate the elusive straw. His dry lips sip.

"I was drafted into the Army after high school and went off to strange places. I always thought, 'When I get back, I'm gonna find that girl and marry her.' But it didn't happen." He coughs. "When I came back, I was accepted into the police academy right away. I was twenty-four. It was a strange time… the early Seventies. You don't remember… too young." His eyes are reminiscent and heavy.

"One night… I saw her. I was working an undercover detail at the Westside Bowl." He pauses for a labored breath. "You know over there on the traffic circle?'

I nod and brush the thick lock of grey from his forehead.

"Dena didn't see me. She was with a date, a boyfriend… she was more beautiful than I remembered, a woman now… of nineteen. I watched them for a while. He wasn't very nice. He was pointing in her face, grabbed her arm and pushed her outside. I followed them…" His voice became a shallow whisper.

I remember pictures of her I'd seen in the paper way back then. Dena had the appearance of a Breck girl, long brown hair and a hint of freckles gave her that wholesome, girl-next-door quality.

"He hit her, opened the door, and threw her in the car. He never saw me." Hap's wheezing concerns me, but I don't want to upset him further by asking him to stop. "I ran up behind him and hit him upside his head with my flashlight before he could open his door. Then…"

A surprised expression comes to his face as he looks in my eyes. "She started screaming at me! 'What did you do? Why did you do that?' I tried to explain… that I saw him hit her… and I couldn't stand for a man treating a woman like that. She said it was none of my business… I tried to tell her who I was… that I'd loved her since I first saw her." A tear ran from the corner of his eye. "She called me psycho… for loving her. For trying to help her? I don't know what happened next. She said she was gonna call the police. I *was* the police." A raspy chuckle made him start coughing again. "She was going to ruin my life because I tried to defend her… because I loved her."

He's agitated and I'm worried. *Maybe I should go?* "The parking lot was empty. No one saw anything. I wrapped my arms around her and covered her mouth. She was so small… so fragile. She kicked and bit my hand but she couldn't scream. I put her in my car and drove out to the lake… by the dam. It was so dark." The door swings open and a nurse waddles in. "Go away!" He attempts to yell, but a dry loud whisper is all that comes out.

"Can you come back?" I ask. "I promise we won't be long." She'll have no part of that.

"No, now come on, Lieutenant, I just need to check your IV." She reaches for the green tube and places it around Hap's head and tucks it back up his nostrils. Hap acquiesces, knowing she'll leave soon. She taps a few buttons. "You okay? Need anything?" Hap shakes his head and she exits.

"I'll come back Hap, you can tell me the rest later. I promise I won't say anything to anyone about this." I unhook my purse from the back of the chair and turn to leave.

"Megan, sit! I have to tell you this... now! Dena wouldn't listen to reason. I tried to tell her that I was protecting her, and if she'd keep quiet everything would be okay. She refused to listen to me, she was hysterical. She kept trying to run away. I don't know how it happened... I held her too tight..." Another wheezing breath. "She stopped breathing, went limp in my arms." Rushing to get the words out and visibly upset, he leans his head back on the pillow. "I tried to get her to breathe again Megan, I swear! I didn't want her to die! I loved her. I was so scared." Tears fill his eyes and spill down his cheeks.

29

"All I could think was I had to hide her body." His words broke into my thoughts of remorse. "I drove toward Mustang Park and noticed a culvert down one of those little roads. I took her clothes off and stuffed her in a drainage pipe." Hap tilts his head back and stares at the ceiling gasping for air. "I'd been in combat, Megan, I knew how fast a body could decompose... guess I figured once she'd been there a few days, animals would find the body and..." Hap rips the tube from around his head and clutches his chest.

"I need to get the nurse." I stand.

"No... I'm... alright. Please let me finish. See, you and I are the same. We killed out of desperation." He fumbles with the tube again, attempting to place it back around his head. I wrap it behind his ears, unsure I understand what he just said.

He situates the plastic back up his nose and inhales a pure deep breath. "I put her clothes in the boathouse near the boots, thinking when Kurt was arrested and they searched the property, all would be found." His frustration manifests in a bout of coughs. "You wouldn't be in such a fix today if the investigators had located all the items we planted. And the egg... Megan, that was great!" A pointed finger wags in my direction.

He saw me put the boots in the boathouse? Is he making fun of me? Patronizing me?

"I figured it out after Kacy, when you got sick. Killing someone is hard, but seeing that body later in such a state is nauseating.

"I know… I've been there, Megan. I've experienced that. I was racked with guilt over what I'd done to Dena. It was all over the news, her parents crying on the TV every night… just wanting their little girl back. They begged and pleaded, 'Just bring our little girl home.'" Hap sighs, not at all mocking Dena's parents. He seems truly distraught and weary.

"I knew *I* could give her back, not alive, but at least they could have closure. So… I got myself assigned to the search area I knew best… where I grew up… and I 'found' their daughter for them. I gave them something to bury."

Stunned and not knowing what to do, I place a hand to the side of his face, he leans into it. "Hap, why are you telling me this?"

"Hush, Megan. We don't have much time." He pulls my hand away and holds it in his lap. "Let me finish. Sylvia and I met a couple of months afterwards and started a *normal* life, a married life. It removed all suspicion from me. Sylvia needed me… and wanted me. I knew there was a question about her mental stability, but her father was an influential man, an oil man with deep pockets." He shifts his weight in the bed and continues. "And… after she lost the baby it was all downhill. She never recovered, but I signed on for the long haul. I promised her father I'd never divorce her." Long wheezing breaths escape him while he pauses.

"I followed you… to the cabin, Megan. Then later when you explained to Sam and me, about Kurt… and how he'd hurt you. Damn, what a bastard! I couldn't let him break your heart twice. You have a good heart. It's a crime… to break a heart so pure." Hap returns my hand to his cheek and places his behind it. "I thought I'd keep an eye on you for awhile. I watched you two make love through the window at the cabin."

So, the time I thought I saw movement outside the window, it was Hap. Thinking about it now, I feel naked, ashamed, sorry he saw me like that, with Kurt. I bow my head.

"I fantasized that it was me... that you'd love me like that." Sliding a finger to my chin he raises my gaze to meet his.

"That night you called me to your house?"

"Yes." I nod.

"I don't know what woke you, but I pulled the screen off. I thought if I scared you enough and sent Jackie to live with you, that would put an end to it, no more killing, no more being with him." He seems embarrassed admitting he was a peeping Tom.

"But at the stock show that afternoon I saw you watching Kurt and April. I could feel the pain in your heart. I wanted to rescue you. That evening I went to the cabin and saw them together. That was the trigger moment for me. I decided to cover you, let you get on with it... get the vengeance so well deserved. We've spent a lot of time together, Megan. You are young Dena all over again for me. For years I've watched you mature into an intelligent, beautiful woman, just out of my reach... wanting you so much, but afraid to reach out and touch." In an effort to breathe, he pulls his shoulder back and lifts his head.

"The fear that you'd reject me like she did so long ago kept me from telling you... I didn't dare imagine what touching you would feel like." He rubs the back of my hand on his temple with closed eyes, and I feel clammy moisture. "Telling you now, I have nothing to lose. When I realized you didn't know April was a threat and it appeared you hadn't planned to do away with her, I had to do it. I followed her from the cabin..." He pauses, gives a deep sigh, and continues. "I stopped her with the flashing lights... and well... I didn't know about the insulin until later. I could've used it." He relaxes and turns away from me. "I tied a few cinder blocks to her so she wouldn't be found, alive or dead. She wasn't supposed to surface, at least not for a while.

You don't need to know more than that." He gazes out the window. The gold hue of the sunset diminishes his paleness, for now.

When I saw April with Kurt at the stock show, did Hap already know about them? I want to ask, but I remain silent.

It's okay Hap, we'll figure all this out and be together. I'll love you forever, and to hell with everyone else.

His proclamation of devotion continues. "If I got this far and Kurt was convicted, I would confess all to you, and then you *couldn't* reject me. You'd be mine, bound to me with a secret. I knew if you didn't already care for me and love me, like I love you, you'd grow to." He rubs his forehead. The golden light softens the lines of time etched in his face. "I'm ashamed to say it now, in my ridiculous fantasy, I was gonna blackmail you into loving me!" He chuckles with the deep smoker's rumble.

"Look at the mess I've become. Who could possibly love this?" He sweeps his hands out.

His words slowly soak in. Hesitant to speak, I struggle for a response that won't confirm or deny my actions in his scenario. "What about your wife?"

Is this being recorded for evidence? Surely not. Hap wouldn't confess to murder to entice me to confess. Would he?

"Sylvia? Sylvia is lost from reality most days. Her brother shuffles her around... not wanting the family money out of his grasp." He's exhausted.

"So why are you telling me all this now?" I ask, puzzled.

"Look at me, darling!" His deep voice bounces around the room with another chuckle and a cough. "I'm not long for this world. The doctors are taking me to surgery tomorrow. It's all I've got, my last shot. I won't make it out alive."

"Don't say that, Hap!" I grip his large cold hands in mine and admit to him. "I should've killed Kurt, I thought about it, ya know. I could've slit his throat and left him lying in that bed. No one would've known."

"Megan, you need to know... Dr. Mann..." He sits straight

up, looks at the door and coughs hard, then grabs my face. "There's not much time. She knows something. She..." he falls back to the soft pillows. "She indicated in her report you may not be so innocent. She attached an addendum to it, suggesting you need psychological counseling. Hinting perhaps you have inner demons and with your history of abandonment... that could manifest into unpredictable tendencies that even you won't be able to control. I haven't told anyone they already have." Hap pants slightly from the effort to make his point.

"The big unanswered question is motive. Why... why would Kurt come back after all these years to murder two women that were nothing to him? The same thing I wondered until I realized he didn't. He came back alright, for you. Not for them. Do you have something he wants, Megan?" Hap grips my wrist with a shudder.

This is my chance to tell Hap about finding the key and the money. I want to tell him what I've done about the letters from Kurt and how frightened I am that I'll be the one in prison before this is over.

"I guess it really doesn't matter now. I destroyed the part of her report that implicates you, but it probably isn't the only copy out there. Watch out for her, Megan, she can hurt you." I don't remember specifically what I said to Dr. Mann for her to interpret my interview any way except Kurt's guilt. He reads the confusion on my face.

"Don't talk to her anymore. Don't talk to anyone. Never talk of this to anyone ever! You know that's how they all get caught." The word brought on another bout of coughing and gasping. "For God's sake, Megan, how many times have we laughed at the idiots for being so stupid. You never break rule number one —keep your mouth shut. Promise me."

"I promise." I didn't tell him I'd already confessed to Kurt in jail and that'll be the crux of his defense. *My words, my big mouth are gonna land me in prison.*

"Now, let me help. Let me love you, let me bury the past and save you."

"It doesn't matter now, Hap." I rest my head on his chest and embrace him. "I do love you. I'll love you forever."

"Now, you'll never speak of this again, but you must confess for absolution before you die. I know you're not religious, but I have to know you'll do that for me, okay?" Catholicism found him.

"Okay, I will. You don't have to do this." I say sobbing.

A soft knock on the door interrupts us.

"In the next few minutes... you just keep your mouth shut. Okay? You do that for me. You let me make some lemonade outta all this piss water. Okay?" His once swimming-pool-water eyes are a dull grey.

"Okay." *What is he up to?*

"You rang, Lieutenant?" Detective Hernandez pushes the door open with a thud. "Geez! I'm sorry, didn't mean to interrupt." He's stunned to see Hap in such a state. "Are you 'bout ready to bust outta this place?" He recovers, not wanting Hap to pick up on his shock at the sight of him.

"No, I won't be leaving here anytime soon. Did you bring the tape recorder?" Hap quizzes the little man.

"Yep, right here... what's up?" Hernandez lifts the small, handheld device from his jacket pocket.

"I've got some talking to do, and you need to listen carefully. Got it?" Hap reaches for his water again and I hold it as he sips. "Turn it on," Hap says, and the detective clicks the button and sets it on the bed tray hovering above Hap's knees.

"I killed those women," Hap blurts out.

"Hey... hey now, wait a minute!" Hernandez punches the stop button and clicks off the recorder. "Are you nuts, old man? Kurt Terrell's trial starts next week. You can't go around saying stuff like that."

"I can and I will... and you're here to take my statement...

my deathbed confession." Hap reaches for the recorder, just beyond his fingertips. "Turn that damn thing back on."

"Well, then... we're gonna do this right." Hernandez reaches around and retrieves his handcuffs from the leather case attached to his belt. He hooks one bracelet on Hap's left wrist and the other to the bed rail.

I stand quickly and yank Hap's hand almost out of his grasp as the cuff ticks in place. "Hey! I don't think that's necessary!"

"Sit down... Megan. It's okay, it's gonna be okay now." Hap pushes my hand away and pats it into the bed linen. Holding his right hand, I sit in disbelief at what the last hour revealed to me. Hap changed the course of my life and in the next minutes he will change Kurt's as well.

My revenge didn't last long. Kurt sat in jail less than two years. Is that enough pay back? Was it ever my decision or my judgment call?

I killed for vengeance. Hap killed for love, misguided love, but not out of hate. After what I've done, I feel like a monster incapable of being loved. Not deserving love. Now in the end someone not only loves me, but professes it, at the end. What kind of love would have you kill to preserve it?

Hernandez points to me. "And... *she* needs to leave."

"No... *she* needs to hear it, all of it. Now turn that thing back on!" Hap coughs and his body shivers.

Click. Hernandez Mirandizes Hap. "Yeah, yeah I waive all rights." He begins his confession of the intricate details of each murder, except Dena's. With detailed knowledge of Kacy's and Missy's deaths, Hap lies convincingly as he spells out the intricate plan in first-person context.

"I flashed my badge and they let me walk right into their homes. Can you believe they both let a complete stranger in because he appeared to be a policeman?"

When he finished, Hernandez had one question. "Why Hap?"

"I couldn't let the bastard hurt her again." He turns to face me. "When I knew he was back, probably hoping the statutes had run out on everything he's done. Megan didn't deserve what he'd already done to her. I couldn't let it happen all over again. I knew how much she still loved him and she'd be easy prey for him. I was protecting Megan." A fat tear broke free falling into a fold of his cotton gown.

The confession of Dena's murder was solely for my benefit, to help me understand why he needed to do this for me. One of the secrets I'll take to my grave. Who am I to question why? If he feels he can right some terrible wrongs before leaving this world, why shouldn't I let him? I lay my arm across his waist and snuggle my shoulder up under his, to that warm familiar place, with my head on his chest. Publicly, but silently, displaying my love, my gratitude for his words. He washed my sins away. His fingers comb my hair as he speaks and I listen as his baritone voice rumbles in cadence with each raspy breath.

Since Kurt's arrest, I've been living scared and exhausted. Hating what I did. Regret a constant weight, knowing that my children and family would suffer the shame of my actions. I couldn't confess and allow myself the sanctuary of prison life or the possibility of an ultimate escape.

"Is that it?" Detective Hernandez places a finger on the stop button. Hap nods. Click.

He leaves the room and I crawl in bed with Hap. At this moment, I feel secure, warm, and loved. Like a child wrapped in the arms of a loving parent as a lullaby of forever love serenades. I drift asleep to the orchestra of noise and harmony of the voices in my head.

I wake briefly as the media announces on the 10 o'clock news that the District Attorney's Office will drop all murder charges against Kurt, citing lack of evidence. "… and with time served, it looks like he'll be released pending the analysis of evidence linking him to the murder of Dena Morgan and a decision by the SEC on past fraud and embezzlement charges." With the wolves at bay, I click off the TV and share peaceful silence with Hap sleeping beside me.

Before dawn, Hap's familiar scent embraces my whole being and his arms shelter me from the world I must face... alone... once again. I listen to each troubled breath as the memories of last evening loop in my head. Hap saved me from a horrific future. A future I brought on myself, fighting for my life and mere glimpses of my loved ones. His words to Hernandez secured my destiny... to see my sons with children.

Sylvia and her entourage will arrive with the sun to sit at Hap's bedside until he's taken off to surgery. I must leave Hap now. Knowing I may never see him again wrenches my heart. The pain in my chest compels my tears to flow uncontrollably.

"I have to go now." I raise my head and look deep in his tired eyes. He is crying also. He pulls my head back to his chest with a squeeze.

"Nobody will ever... love you enough, Megan," Hap whispers. "Not enough... to make up for what Kurt did to you... and for the love I couldn't show you." A tear rolls to the edge of the green tubing and down his cheek.

I prop myself on both knees to face him and hold his face in my hands. Our eyes lock... our souls pair for eternity, accepting the possibility of a harsh punishment in the afterlife.

"Please don't leave me." Fruitless whispered words echoed from my past render Hap powerless. I brush away his tears and hold him close one last time as sobs rise from my thawed heart. I gather my jacket and purse, pull the door open, and look back to see his outstretched hand as he mouths the words, *I love you*.

I walk past the uniformed officer sitting at Hap's door, down the corridor into the dawn. Hap was right... he never returned from the operating room. The bagpipes escorted him home.

THE MELANCHOLY TUNE drones and whines, changing pitch with each breath. I lean on a large oak tree and watch the full military regalia of a police funeral at a distance from others seated graveside. Sylvia's outstretched arms and spindly fingers draw the red, white, and blue triangle in to her chest. Three towering antennas atop news vans parked in line behind the progression of vehicles will broadcast Hap's formal farewell.

IN MY MIND'S eye I see Kurt lying on the top bunk in his cell. The stress has aged his now pale face as hopeless eyes gaze at nothing. Detective Hernandez gathers the portrait pictures of the three murdered women, opens the large accordion file and drops them and the cassette tape in, closes the flap and stuffs the folder into a file cabinet drawer. A tattered file labeled D. Morgan lays on his desk.

ED AND JACKIE walk from the graveside arm in arm. My tall brother embraces me, and I breathe him in. The three of us walk toward the car. He opens the rear door for me, then the front for Jackie. As I lean to get in, a heavy brass key sways from a chain around my neck. Ed fastens his seatbelt and lovingly wipes a tear from Jackie's cheek. He pats her belly and turns to me with a bittersweet smile. The shade cast from tall oak trees dapples our path as we drive away.

Hap's confession is innocuously placed in the open case files of the dead women. Information contained in unsolved homicides is unavailable to the public.

30

"Grandma! Grandma! Look what I found!" I'm amazed, the redheaded twelve-year-old is as tall as me. She holds a large green beetle upside down as its legs flail about. "Its belly glows." Even in the fading light of another spectacular sunset, the iridescent stomach glimmered.

"I looked it up on my phone." She reads from the display. "It's a Con... Continis mu... mu-ta-bilis." She stumbled with the pronunciation. "Also known as a Figeater, it's commonly mistaken for a Japanese beetle; however, they do not damage lawns and fruit crops like their eastern cousins."

I pause to absorb the sweetness of the broad smile enhancing her freckled face. Katy Rae possesses the old soul of her namesake and the analytical mind of her grandmother, the scientist. "Katy put that poor creature back where you found it."

Connor approaches us and gives me a sideways hug in one arm as the toddler squirms for release from the other. With a kiss for my son and a pinch to the cheek of his, I reach to embrace my handsome nephew, Hap.

As the party winds to a close, Father Galindo cups my elbow, directing me away from the crowd and strands of twinkling lights to the meditation bench facing the beach. "Your home is full of all your loved ones?"

"Yes, my home and my heart are full of my loved ones, living and not." I look at my freshly pedicured toes and wiggle them in the sand.

"Señora, you look so happy. Are you at peace?"

"Yes, Father, I am finally at peace."

AUTHOR'S NOTE

Abandoned in a world of debt by my fugitive husband, I desperately hung on to the hope that an education would rescue my son and me. My psychology professor, knowing my sufferings, asked me, "What would you do if he came back?" Thus, this story was conceived and birthed through the pain of betrayal and the loss of true love's innocence.

I'd like to acknowledge Max Courtney and Dana E. Austin, Ph.D. for their tutelage and belief in my abilities as a forensic scientist. To Jason Myers, Jeff Posey and the numerous DFW Writers' Workshop members, thank you for the critiques and encouragement to put more pen to paper.

Special hugs for my mom, Seth, Melissa, Clint, Jason and Talana—thank you for teaching me how to overcome life's obstacles with agility and grace.

This story would not exist without the actions of Jaylynn Timothy Baxter. You know what you did.

.

If you enjoyed this book and would like to support the creation of additional tales, please do one or more of the following:

- Leave a review on your favorite book review site
- Tell a friend about *Shambles*
- Ask your local library to put *Shambles* on the shelf
- Recommend titles by Fawkes Press to your local bookstore

VISIT US ONLINE
WWW.FAWKESPRESS.COM

FAWKES PRESS